André Tom Macgregor

André Tom Macgregor

BETTY WILSON

6477

Macmillan of Canada
Toronto

ISBN 0-7705-1329-8

Printed in Canada for
The Macmillan Company of Canada
70 Bond Street, Toronto M5B 1X3

André Tom Macgregor

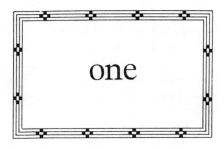

one

André Tom Macgregor cautiously opened the door and stepped out of Albert Rose's shack. It was July, but the red plaid bush shirt he had pulled over his nakedness did not relieve the chill of the northern Alberta night.

"André, baby, where the hell you goin'?" Dodie Rose called, her voice thick with sleep. "Told you that bastard of an Albert won't be home till tomorrow."

"Nowhere I ain't comin' back from."

He grinned. Great piece of ass, that.

"But — "

"Save your strength. You're gonna need it."

She giggled. "Four times tonight? Jeez! Takes a seventeen-year-old kid to show these guys that think they're such stud horses."

"You ain't seen nothin' yet."

He stepped with bare-footed caution into the moon-shadow beside the shack, where he urinated long and urgently against the dull silver glow of Albert Rose's propane tank.

Lucky bastard, that Rose. Propane. Shack's as warm as Dodie's tits, winter and summer.

He scowled across the fence at his father's shack with its slatted-down tar-paper siding.

Wonder when the government'll get around to building us something decent, and drilling us a well? Lamp's still burning. Hell of a long stook game. Hope the old man's winning. If he ain't, there goes the welfare cheque, and Ma never bought grub. Out of tea and sugar — He sighed. Be on my back for more than board when I get paid tomorrow night.

He waited in the moon-shadow, senses straining. Watch it. Somebody spot me and blab to Albert Rose that I'm balling his old lady—He shivered. Seen that bastard kick the living shit out of Harold Kusak outside of the beer parlor that time—

When he was certain that nothing moved in the night he sprinted for Rose's door, bare legs and feet slashed by icy, couch grass wet with dew.

"Lemme in the little old sack. Got somethin' for you besides cold feet!" he crowed as he slammed the door behind him.

"Shhh! You tryin' to tell the whole town?"

"'Cause I slammed the door? You pee in the middle of the night."

"Yeah, but I use the slop pail."

He shucked his shirt, yanked back the covers, dived into the bed, and grabbed her.

"You bastard!" she shrieked. "Them feet'd freeze the balls off a brass monkey." She hit him alongside the ear with her fist. "Bloody breed! Get outta this bed. What the hell d'ya think I am?"

He caught her other fist and backed off, dragging the covers with him.

"That's right! Freeze me with your stinkin' wet feet, then drag all the blankets off. Jesus!"

André scrambled out of the bed and stood naked; hurt, then suddenly angry.

"You don't like breeds, eh? Seen Jake Strugglin' Eyes and Alex Mulligan leavin' this shack at some pretty funny hours when Albert was away on long hauls last winter."

There was a pause filled with her agitated breathing. "Ah, honey, I'm sorry. C'mon, I'll warm your feet and—"

A dismal wail rose from the crib in the corner of the room.

"God! Now we've woke the kid. Get in and lay down. Maybe if we're quiet—"

André hesitated, then lay rigidly beside her, not touching her. The baby's howls of outrage changed to shuddery sobs of fright.

Poor little bugger. Ain't she gonna—?

Dodie leaned across him, her breasts dragging across his chest, and kissed him hungrily. "What's that about you had somethin' for me?" she crooned. Her breath was sour with beer and cigarette smoke.

"What about the kid?"

"Hell with him. He's only cuttin' teeth." Her mouth fastened on his, tongue exploring as one hand smoothed its way down his flank.

His desire had evaporated. He felt tired, impotent, and rather silly. The baby's crying troubled him. He grabbed the hand creeping down toward his groin and wrenched his mouth away from hers.

"Sorry. Guess I'm just — " He broke off on a snort of embarrassed laughter and cleared his throat. The baby continued to cry.

"Aw, sweetie, did I hurt your feelin's? But honest, I can't stand cold feet. I'll settle the kid down, then maybe — "

She sat up, stretching like a sleepy cat. Her flesh glowed in the moonlight and he could see the deep purple nipples of her breasts. She shivered, sprang from the bed, and crossed the room to the whimpering baby.

"What's wrong with *you*? Phew! What a time to crap! Lay down, goddamnit. Don't want it all over the bed." She turned to André. "Couple of beers left in the case. Help yourself. Be a while cleanin' this brat."

Beer? Hell with it. Wanna sleep, but when she's through with the kid—Wish I never opened my big mouth before I went out to pee. She wants it. And I couldn't no more than—Gotta think of something to tell her so I can sneak back to the old man's shack. Something that don't make me look too stupid —

The dilemma was solved for him by a swathe of light cutting around three sides of the room as a heavy gravel truck rumbled and jounced into the yard.

"Jesus Christ! It's Albert!" Dodie gasped.

André didn't need to be told. He blundered about grabbing clothes in the dim light, whimpering like a dog that knows it is about to be beaten.

"Never mind gettin' dressed," Dodie hissed. "Grab your clothes and duck out the back door." She peered out of the window. "Hurry! He's comin'."

"Can't find one shoe."

"Oh, for christsake — *There!* On the chair."

He grabbed the shoe and scampered for the back door. As his hand closed on the knob she was onto him like a clawing cat.

"Don't! Wash tub's blockin' the way. I forgot to dump it."

He ripped away from her, almost losing his armful of clothes, opened the inner door and set his shoulder to the screen to force the tub out of the way.

"No! He'll hear the clatter."

"Leggo!"

"We got a second. He stopped to talk to Johnny Crane and Willie Averil out in your dad's yard. Get under the bed. Albert's a heavy sleeper. When he starts to snore — "

André dived under the bed and lay with his face pressed to the dirty linoleum, heart hammering and body a-quiver, hoping desperately that he had all his clothes still gathered in the crook of his arm.

"Bastard'll spot me. I know he will." He opened his mouth to quiet the sound of his ragged breathing and squeezed his eyes shut.

"The bed, Dodie — It's a mess. He'll know — "

"Shhh! I'll fix it."

She was standing beside the bed, her big toe almost touching his nose. As he heard her gag, a monstrous black shadow crossed the window. Dodie heaved, and he heard the rushing sound of vomit. He knew she'd stuck her fingers down her throat.

Heavy boots mounted the doorstep. "See you guys when the duck huntin' season opens," Albert called back to the men in the yard. "Right now my ass is draggin'!"

Dodie was gasping sickly and dragging the foul sheets from the bed when Albert kicked the door open. The light snapped on, and the room sprang into harsh, brilliant light. André's terror drove him to the deeper shadow against the wall, where his hand scrabbled through a mess of fresh cat shit.

"What the hell's goin' on here?" Albert demanded.

"Albert, am I glad to see you! I been heavin' my guts out all day, an' that kid's been — "

"You been sloppin' beer again, I can smell it."

He clomped across to the crib where the baby hiccuped on sobs. "Wassa matter fella? Can't your old lady keep a clean didy on your ass, and see you're covered up so you don't freeze at night?"

He picked the baby up and carried him to the rocking chair beside the heater.

"I *was* cleaning him up when — "

4

"Oh, sure! Bet you never even give him his supper."

"I sure as hell did. Whaddya think — ?"

"Think I'm goddamn good an' sick of comin' home from a four day trip an' finding the kid bawlin' an' you sloppin' beer. Now, get that bed made. I've had four hours sleep in the last day an' a half."

When Albert began to gag on his own snoring, André inched out from under the bed. As he closed the door he heard Dodie choking back a titter. Once clear of the step, he sprinted for the picket fence that poked up here and there in the forest of couch grass, cleared it — and landed with his bare foot on a shard of broken beer bottle. On the toes of one foot and the heel of the other, he hobbled into his father's shack, trailing blood.

Isaac Macgregor was sitting on a straight-backed chair in the moonlight, his arms folded on the square of worn plastic that covered the kitchen table. His heavily seamed face looked full Indian in that light.

"Rose catch you with his woman, and your balls be danglin' from a spruce tree," he said in Cree. He shoved the chair back and padded across to the bed in the corner.

André set his clothes on the chair Isaac had vacated.

Should light the lamp and take a look at this fucking cut. Bleeding like a stuck pig. But wake Ma up, and she'll raise hell. I'll pack the lamp back into Chickadee's cubby-hole and light it there. Chickybird's a good kid. Wouldn't care — Oh, Christ! Simone's sleeping with Chicky. Forgot. Wake that bitch up and — Hell with it. Only a glass cut. Nothing to what Albert Rose'd done to me if he caught me.

He took a towel from the nail, wrapped it tight around his injury, and hobbled to the bed. As he picked up his alarm clock he glanced apprehensively toward Rachel, his mother, sleeping beside Isaac. He shoved the clock under the pillow to stifle the sound as he wound it, pulled the alarm button, and set it on the floor.

Ma sure hates that clock. Always giving me shit 'cause she don't like the sound of it ticking, and bugging me for letting a machine boss me around. And the alarm — Wow! When that wakes her up —

He eased his bandaged foot under the tangle of blankets and stretched out beside Joey, Simone's six-year-old bastard.

5

two

A woodpecker hammering on the tin chimney wakened him in the morning.

Bugger! Enough to deafen a guy, and Ma never twitched an eyebrow. Now, if it was the clock —

He reached down and pushed in the alarm button. He was so weary his bones felt rotten. His foot burned and throbbed, but he swung his legs over the side of the bed and unwrapped the towel. His jaws clenched as he examined the cut.

Needs stitches. And I gotta stand all day to pump gas and wash windshields. Hell with it. Ain't going.

He lay back on the bed, mocking himself with an imagined conversation between his employer and his priest.

"Gave young Macgregor a chance 'cause you asked me to, Father," Bill Mason said, "but he's a breed. You know you can't count on any of 'em."

"Clever lad, Mr. Mason. I have high hopes for him."

Old bastard! Hell with it. They can't claim I'm goofing off today. Not with a cut like this.

But it's Saturday. Olsons'll be in at the garage, sure as hell. That Dolores is giving me the eye. Cut, or no cut, I ain't passing that up.

He got to his feet, heeled it across to the nail where the dish towel was hung, and ripped a strip off the end of it to use for a bandage.

At the sound of ripping cloth, Rachel heaved from her back to her backside. "What're you doin'?"

"Cut my foot."

"Where was you last night?"

6

He shrugged. She knows where I was.

She giggled behind her palm. "Dat Rose bitch payin'?"

He turned his back on her, pulled a dirty sock over the bandage, and eased into a canvas running shoe. When he put his weight on the foot he felt it begin to bleed.

"You wash my other shirt and pants?"

"What's wrong with them?" She stabbed her finger in the direction of the pile of clothes he had left on the chair.

He made a wry face as he sorted out the rumpled shirt with a gob of dried cat crap stuck to one sleeve. He took a table knife and scraped the offending mess into the cold kitchen stove, then pulled the shirt on.

Don't smell so good, but — Ah, to hell with it.

He went to the rough shelves where Rachel kept the food. "Any bread?"

"Bread? Ho!" Her voice was shrill with resentment. "You want bread, Mr. Rich-White-Man, you buy it."

"I'm payin' board."

"Board, shit! You think it's right you pay a liddle board and du rest of us go hungry when you got money? What way is dat? Dumb white man way!"

"Ain't my idea. Father Pépin says — "

"If dat goddamn priest says your pecker's your nose you try to blow it, huh?"

He ran a comb through his lank, black hair, and escaped into the brilliant, dew-wet morning.

She think it's fun for me, cooped up in that goddamn garage all summer? Look at the lake! Man! Out by Frenchman's Bay pelicans'll be nesting on the rocks. And cormorants. And I ain't even seen 'em.

Pelicans — Shit! Never see the *guys*. *They're* fishing, or chasing women, or just laying on their backs in the sun. I'm a stupid bastard. Wish I had the guts to tell that old fart of a priest to mind his own business. Brain in my head, he says. Shit!

The town of Fish Lake, population slightly less than eight hundred, stretched for a mile along the lake. Its one main street, the lakeshore road, had never been paved. Only the business section — three stores, a hotel, two garages, and a movie theatre — could even boast sidewalks. From the Métis settlement on the northern fringes of town to Bill Mason's garage was slightly more than half a mile. That morning it seemed farther, much farther.

He arrived at the service station as Bill Mason was unlocking the door. Mason, a lanky fellow with hard blue eyes and a grizzled, upstanding mop of hair, paused with the key still in the lock and looked him up and down.

"What's wrong with your foot?" He crouched abruptly, a frown between his brows. "Jesus! Your shoe's dripping blood."

"Little cut. Bleedin' a lot."

Mason rose and opened the door of the service station. "Let's have a look."

Reluctantly, André followed him inside and bared his foot for inspection.

"Think you're gonna work with *that*?" Mason snorted. "You're going straight to the hospital for stitches."

"It'll quit bleedin'."

"Get Doc Pêche to fix you up. If he says you can work today, okay. Otherwise—" He wrinkled his nose. "What the hell you been into? Cat shit?

"Now, look—When you're out there pumping gas you represent this service station. In other words, *me*. I don't come to work plastered with cat shit. Take the pick-up. Get yourself over to the hospital. And don't show up here till you're decent."

What I get for fooling around with Dodie Rose. Stupid bitch don't even treat her kid right. If Ma was burning, Dodie Rose wouldn't pee on her, but no kid at our place bawled alone in the middle of the night. Hell with Dodie Rose. I ain't going back there.

But he knew he would. Sooner or later.

It was eleven o'clock before he returned to the service station. His stitched and bandaged foot was covered with a scrubbed running shoe, still slightly damp, and he wore freshly laundered clothes.

Mason grinned at him sardonically. "More like it. Now, get to work."

The garage was a hive of activity that Saturday. Mason had no time for his pet project, a genuine 1917 Tin Lizzie he was restoring to drive in the rodeo parade at the end of August. But it was on his mind.

"Sure hope Ole Olson shows up today," he fretted to André.

"Gotta dicker the old bugger out of them wooden-spoked wheels he's got out on his place. Don't dare go out there. He knew how bad I wanted 'em, he'd be askin' sixty dollars apiece."

Screw the wheels. Just as long as the old boy brings Dolores with him. André's crotch swelled and warmed. Boy! If I can get her off by herself—

At half-past four the ancient Olson farm truck pulled in beside the gas pumps. As he gassed up the Olson vehicle André was pricklingly aware of Dolores lolling on a bench in the truck box. He glanced up to meet her cat-green eyes. She winked at him and pursed her lips in a whisper of a wolf whistle.

Hot blood rushed into his face. He glanced covertly into the cab of the truck, where Ole was squinting at the gauges on the gas pump while Mrs. Olson, hollow-cheeked and dead-eyed, examined black work-cracks in her palms. Only Astrid, the teen-aged mongoloid sitting between her parents, watched André, but with blank, unaware eyes.

Dolores, noting his appraisal of her family, giggled in a suppressed, silent spasm. But when Ole suddenly stepped out of the truck to greet Bill Mason, it was as if an invisible sponge had wiped all expression from her face, leaving it blank and bored.

"Dolores."

"Yes, Daddy?" she answered with the anxious deference of an over-disciplined little child.

"Get the truck outta the way when the kid's finished cleaning the windshield. I wanna talk to Bill."

"Okay, Daddy. Sure," she agreed in a high-pitched chirp.

When Ole turned away, her eyes narrowed and she stuck a long tongue out at his retreating back. She rose, hopped from the truck and landed, breast to chest with André, in a lithe, knee-bent spring. Her eyes held his. When he finally dropped his gaze she giggled.

For the next half-hour she wandered about the lot striking gauche, and faintly suggestive, poses for André's benefit. Mrs. Olson snoozed, and the mongoloid turned a red ball of wool over and over in her pudgy hands.

At last Bill and Ole came out of the garage.

"You'll be driving down to St. Paul Monday, Dolores," Ole said.

"You can take the engine outta that old Pontiac my brother's driving if he lets you use his hoist, can't you, André?" Mason asked.

"Yeah, sure."

"That's it, then. You'll go with Dolores." Mason turned and pumped Ole's hand. "Beat me on the deal, you old rascal, but I'm gonna have me an honest-to-god restored Model T to drive in the parade."

André's heart thumped. He eyed Dolores' neatly rounded backside as she climbed into the box of the truck. Her green eyes held his as the truck moved away.

"Man! That Dolores — "

"Don't get ideas," Mason said sharply. "Ole's getting along, maybe, but he's a tough old bugger. He'd crucify the guy that looked cross-eyed at her."

"Not me that's got the ideas."

By closing time André was squeamish from the pain in his foot. He washed mud from the windshield of the last farm truck, and counted change into the calloused hand of the driver. Bill Mason let him through the already locked door of the service station, and counted his wages out of the till.

"Run you home," he offered.

"Gotta wait for Father Pépin."

"Oh, yeah. Keep forgetting he's saving your wages for you." He examined André curiously. "Are you really going out to Edmonton to university or technical school in September?"

"Oh, jeez! Father keeps sayin', but — I dunno — "

Mason leaned on the counter and looked through the plate glass window. "Your Ma's waiting for you. If she gets her claws into you before Father Pépin shows up, that's one week's wages you ain't gonna save."

Rachel skulked down the sidewalk on the other side of the street. Though the day was hot, she wore a parka zipped to the throat, a dirty red bandana tied over her hair, and moccasins covered by old rubbers. Hands deep in her parka pockets, she shuffled twenty feet down the street, stopped, glanced at the service station, turned, and shuffled twenty feet back.

"Wanna sneak out the back way?"

"Nah. Father Pépin's comin'."

He bobbed his head at Bill Mason and went out to meet the priest who bustled across the service station lot, dusty cassock flapping about his ankles, and white whiskers quivering. He thrust back his head to examine André through the magnifying portion of his bi-focals.

"'Allo, André. 'Allo. The first day of August tomorrow," the priest bubbled.

"Huh?"

"The examination results. The official marks! In the mail now — Any day. You have decided which of the sciences you wish to study?"

"Jeez, Father! S'pose—Well, even s'pose I wanna—Well, jeez, who's gonna hand it to *me*? I'm Métis. It's them damn treaty guys that get—".

"You wish to go?" Father Pépin interrupted.

He's crazy! Me study two or three years on what I earn working as a pump jockey in the summer—He carefully blanked his face and shrugged.

"I 'ave the brochures for you. Northern Alberta Institute of Technology, and the university. I will take you to the rectory now, and—"

Before André could protest further, Rachel was upon them. "What you take my kid's money for, Fadder? Me, I got nothin' to buy grub."

"Take?" the priest snapped indignantly. "I *save* it for 'im!" He scowled at her. "You 'ave been cut off welfare?"

She scuffed through the dust with the toe of her rubber and muttered sullenly, "Isaac goes to du beer parlor."

"You say to me *you* don't?"

"Don't play stook anyhow. That Johnny Crane and Willie Averil, dey cleaned him. Every cent."

The priest's lips compressed and breath whistled in his nostrils. "Go to the store when the welfare cheque comes, eh? Then you can buy the grocery for the month."

She cast a look of black hostility at André. "Him! Money — And du kids go wid empty bellies."

"'e pays 'is board today."

"Board! Yeah—"

Father Pépin imperiously thrust the palm of his hand under André's nose. André extracted the week's wages from his pocket and dropped the crumpled bills into the priest's hand.

Brows beetling, Father Pépin flattened and sorted the money, counting with moving lips.

"Eight dollars you are short?"

"Missed work this morning."

"*Missed work?* When I get you this job I tell you — "

"I know what you told me."

Father Pépin's eyes narrowed. "This week you do without the spending allowance."

Old bastard! Whose money — ? Jeez! It's me that's crazy!

Hot with resentment he watched the priest count forty dollars' board money into Rachel's hand, then fold the rest and stuff it into an old-fashioned leather snap purse.

Saving it for me! What if he says I never give him no money? Oh shit! I know better, but —

Rachel crumpled the money in her palm, cast a look of scorn at André and shuffled off toward the grocery store, the shapeless bulk of her body carried on too-thin shapeless legs. Joey burst out of a clump of willows at the far side of the street and scampered after her.

The priest's eyes followed them disapprovingly before he turned to André. "Come to the rectory with me. The brochures — "

Goddamn brochures! He shook his head.

"Can't I make you understand. It is most important that you — "

"How'm I gonna go to them places? Just tell me."

The priest smiled slyly and jogged him in the ribs with his elbow. "The English 'ave a saying — 'Where there is a will, there is a way'."

Oh, Christ! More crap —

"Father, maybe I go home now. Don't feel so good."

"Then I will speak with you after Mass tomorrow!" It was an order. The priest walked away, slammed into his car, and disappeared in a spiral of dust.

Never even offered to drive me home!

Grunting with pain at every step, he hobbled off toward the Métis settlement overlooking the lake at the edge of town.

three

Dodie Rose, dressed in skin-tight pants and a see-through blouse with no brassière underneath it, was pretending to weed the few, sickly rows of vegetables in her garden when André came home. She picked her way through the couch grass and thistles to the edge of the picket fence. André flapped a hand at her by way of greeting and was about to enter the shack without speaking to her, when she called across:

"Hey, André!"

Reluctantly he hobbled toward her.

"What's wrong with your foot?"

"Sliced it on a busted beer bottle when I jumped the fence last night."

She laughed shrilly. "Jesus! If that's all—I'll never forget you sneakin' through the door with your bare ass hangin' out when Albert started to snore."

He laughed. "Better make sure you get your wash tub dumped after this."

"Well, he took off again. Won't be back till Thursday night." She wiggled her backside. "I could fix you some bacon and eggs."

He plucked a long stem of couch grass and nipped it off, section by section. "Not tonight. I'm beat."

Out of the corner of his eye he saw Rachel come up to the shack, a bag of groceries in her arms. She went in and banged the door behind her without looking at them.

André backed away from the fence.

"Aw, c'mon, André."

"Nah. I'm pooped. And I gotta go to Mass tomorrow morning."

"Mass? Jesuschrist!" Her face went taut with suspicion. "Goin' to confession? Goddamn you, you spread anythin' around about me that gets back to Albert and I'll — "

"Father Pépin don't blab," he said, grinning at her as he limped away.

As he mounted the broken stoop of Isaac's shack he noticed Aubrey Sladden's old Ford parked out beside the privy. He made a wry face and pushed the door open in time to hear Aubrey's outraged protest, "Five dollars for you, Isaac, and five for Simone. Now, Jesuschrist — "

"Seven for du old man, and seven for me," Simone bargained. She flung herself into Sladden's lap and caressed his ear with the tips of her fingers. Sladden shoved her away and crossed his knees with a snort of embarrassed laughter.

Simone giggled behind her palm. "Two bucks ain't nothin' when you need a woman that bad, Sladden."

Unnoticed, André sidled in and sat down on the edge of the bed where he eased the shoe off his throbbing foot.

"Deal, Sladden?" Simone wheedled.

Rachel was at the stove, scrubbing pots in a dishpan full of greasy water, a black frown on her face. She swung around on Simone, jowls quivering. "Joey comin' pretty soon. What way is dat for him to see his modder?" She gestured toward Isaac with the dripping pot. "You — pimpin'! Got no shame?"

"Holy shit! Think I'm Mr. Moneybags? Simone runs off and don't tell du social worker in dat Edmonton. Gets kicked off welfare. We s'posed to keep her? Me, I got no job — "

"Johnny Evans at the feed lot asked you — "

"Shut your fat mouth!" He gathered himself to spring at her.

Rachel retreated to the door. "Shit!" she spat at Isaac. "You, Simone, you got no shame to go wid a bastard like dat?" She gestured with the pot toward Sladden.

"Huh! What about you and Jake Fish Eye? And dat Jimmy guy before you got fat and ugly?"

Rachel fired the pot at her. Simone ducked and the pot clattered against the stove.

"You got no shame!" Rachel shouted. She went out, slamming the door so hard that André winced.

Simone swung around, half-sitting on the table, weight on her hands behind her so that her breasts were sharply defined under her blouse. "We got a deal, Sladden?"

Sladden's tongue passed around the perimeter of his lips. "Six for you, and six for Isaac."

Isaac's expression was sly. "Simone say seven."

Simone slipped off the table and peered into the distorted square of the mirror that hung over the wash stand. She began to smear lipstick on her mouth. Aubrey twisted around to watch her. "Aw, c'mon, baby. I brung a bottle of wine. We'll drive down by Frenchman's Bay, and — "

Simone giggled, picked up a dirty comb with several teeth missing, and yanked it through the tangles of a cheap home-permanent. "Seven dollar," she insisted, "And gimme a smoke."

Sladden sighed, took a packet of Exports from his breast pocket and tossed them on the table. She took one, lit it with a kitchen match, and flipped the open pack down in front of Isaac. He helped himself without permission.

Simone came and leaned against Sladden, toying with the hair at the nape of his neck. "I zig-zig good," she murmured. He gulped, his face strained with desire, as he got to his feet. "All right, goddamn it, seven for you and—"

"Ten for me," Isaac put in.

"Jesuschrist! You said — "

"Ten. Gotta eat."

"Isaac, you chisellin' old bastard — "

"Ten."

Sladden's beer belly bulged over his belt as he went deep into his pants pocket and brought out a roll of bills. Muttering curses, he wet his tongue on his thumb, counted out the money and slapped it on the table. Before Isaac could touch the pile, Simone snatched out seven ones and stuffed them down into her brassière. She turned to Sladden and threw her arms around his neck, allowing her cigarette to fall unheeded to the floor, and slowly rotated her pelvis against him. "C'mon, okay?"

Sladden stumbled through the door, dragging her by the wrist. The car engine roared outside.

Isaac pocketed the money. With the aid of his hands flattened on the table, he lifted himself to his feet, and went to the corner. He fished a greasy parka out of the pile of clothing flung there, and shrugged into it. There was a suggestion of a grin on his face as he closed the door behind him.

Beer parlor. Ma'll follow him down, squabble with him, then

drink more beer than he does. Jeez! I'm hungry. Nothing but a bag of potato chips and three bottles of pop today.

He rummaged through the food shelves.

Tin of baking powder, half a bag of Robin Hood flour, and a pail of lard—Sugar and tea in the bag Ma fetched home. Could make bannock, but I'd have to light the stove—

Joey stepped in out of the dusk. His black eyes took in the room in one wary sweep as he stopped just inside the door, fists deep in bulging pants pockets. He grinned at André. From one pocket he extracted a bag of peanuts; from the other, a bag of Licorice All Sorts.

"Wanna eat, André?"

"Ma buy you that stuff?"

"Nah!"

"Old Fairfax catch you snitchin', he'll call the Mountie."

"Ain't scared of that bastard."

"You better be."

Joey shrugged. "Ma snitched a bottle of Coke." He set his teeth into the plastic bag covering the nuts and ripped, spat the piece of plastic onto the floor, poured a handful of nuts, shoved them into his mouth, and said through them, "Never stole nothin' when you was a little kid, huh?"

André was saved from a reply when Chickadee burst through the door. She was holding three good sized fish from a wire passed through their gills. Except for the thick black braids she flipped back over her shoulders, it would have been hard to tell whether she was a boy or a girl.

"Look at 'em!" she crowed, "Jack, and two pickerel."

She flung her catch onto the table.

"Wow! What a day. Max and me went clean to the other side of the lake. He got a trout. Twenty-three pounds. Fought it half an hour. And you know that Garnet Beach they talk about? The sand is pink. Really pink." She bounced across to André, dived one hand into her pocket and brought forth a palmful of sand. "See? Brought it for your rock collection. Whole pocketful."

André examined the sand minutely, heart quickening with pleasure. "Jeez! How about that?"

"There's an empty tobacco can with the lid on it out by the shit house. You can keep the sand in there until you fix your rock collection. Go fetch it, Joey. Okay?"

"No way," Joey protested. "Gettin' dark out. I'm scared of the weetigo."

"Weetigo, shit!" André snorted, "Who's been fillin' you with them old scary yarns?"

Chickadee's eyes flared with black fright. "Who says they're yarns? Ma says she *seen* her, and Granny told me — "

"Cut it out, Chicky! Whadda you think Sister Bridget'd say if she heard — ?"

"Okay. You ain't scared of the weetigo, you go get the can."

"Stupid bloody—" But when he stepped into the deep night, it took a real effort to keep from looking over his shoulders. He could see the tobacco can shining in the shaft of lamplight coming from the open door of the shack; as he reached down to pick it up, a whistle of duck wings passing overhead raised the hair at the nape of his neck.

Jeez! I dunno — Rock collection, and Father yapping at me about studying science, and I'm scared just as shitless of the old spook yarns as Granny was.

He snatched up the can and hobbled as quickly as he could back to the shack. His heart pounded.

Damn fool! I *know* there's no old woman that's gonna eat me, but —

"Didn't you guys even have supper?" Chicadee asked as she emptied her pocket of sand. "Well, holy jumpin'—! C'mon, Joey, get the fire goin'."

She grabbed the butcher knife and set to work skinning and filleting the fish. Pee Dog apologized his way out from under a bed and approached the table with hopeful eyes.

Chickadee chopped a fillet of jackfish in half and flopped it on the floor in front of him. The skinny pup snatched the fish and scuttled under Isaac's bed as though he expected somebody to take it from him again. Chickadee scraped the leavings of her butchering into the slop pail and rinsed her fish-slimy hands in a cold pan of water.

"I brung home the bacon. You guys cook it."

"Aw, Chicky, c'mon!"

"No way."

André sighed, took the black cast iron frying pan from the nail where it hung, scraped a dollop of lard into it, and set it on the stove. While he rolled the fish in a dish of flour, Chickadee stood on tip-toe, leaning toward the mirror. When she turned and struck a mock-seductive pose, her lips and eyelids were plastered with Simone's make-up.

"How do I look?"

"Wipe your mouth, and get that goddamm chicken shit off your eyes. Old man sees you actin' like that, and next time Sladden comes lookin' for a woman — "

"Screwin's fun. Simone says."

"Fuck Simone! Crazy whore! Screwin's fun, but her? Sleep with a wolverine with the mange if she figured he had five bucks she could get her claws on."

"Well, like the old man says, gotta eat."

four

It was thunder weather the next Monday morning when André appeared at the garage. Mason, a fixed grin on his already oil-smudged face, scarcely glanced at him. His attention was on his prize; what remained of Ole Olson's Model T.

"Look at them wheels!" he crowed. "Honest-to-god wooden spokes. Scarce as hen's teeth. Windshield's okay, and rad's in good shape. Get the best parts of this, and the best parts of mine, and I'm gonna have me a beauty."

He stepped back from the car, still eyeing it as he fished a twenty dollar bill out of his pocket. "Dolores is on her way. Ole just phoned. He says she'll give you a hand with the job, being as my brother's fixing a guy's combine. Tools there in the gunny sack. Now, the two of youse get yourselves a good dinner—"

"Ain't you got somethin' smaller than a twenty?"

"Well, hell! Bring me the change." He glanced at André, then grinned slyly. "Gonna have a bitch of a time keeping your head on the job with Dolores helping." He sobered then. "Feel kinda sorry for the poor kid. Ole keeps her on the farm and treats her like a six-year-old. Only she ain't. She's suffering from a bad case of the hots, but if you know what's good for you, you'll keep your pecker zipped in your pants."

A truck horn blatted. André hoisted the tool sack and went out to climb in the truck beside Dolores. After her performance outside the garage on Saturday night, he didn't know what to expect, but she glanced at him shyly, a tremulous, tentative smile coming and going on her lips.

"Dunno how much good I'll be working on that car," she offered, "but I help Daddy with the farm machinery."

He glanced at her hands on the steering wheel. They were as coarse-grained and hard looking as a stone mason's, the nails deeply bitten.

"Might be me that's helpin' you."

Knows how to drive, he thought when they were a few miles down the highway. And she can keep quiet. I was scared she wouldn't shut her yap all day.

He relaxed to watch hawks hovering on the windward side of the road, watching for mice and gophers frightened into revealing their whereabouts by the passing cars. Poplar leaves flickered, silver-bellied in the wind, and distances shimmered with heat.

Miles had rolled under the truck before Dolores asked, "You still in high school?"

"Finished in June."

"Twelve?"

"Yeah."

"Wow!" She sounded envious. "Daddy made me quit in grade eleven. I wasn't much good at school anyhow."

"Sooner be on the farm, huh?"

"Farm? I hate it. Boy! That Thorvald, he's lucky. No cow manure on *his* boots — "

"Who's that? Thorvald—?"

"My brother. Been teaching in Edmonton for three years." She shifted her slender body into a more comfortable position, and lapsed into silence, her lips drooping pensively. The truck topped a hill, and the country suddenly opened into blue and intriguing distance. "Look at that!" Dolores exclaimed. "Gee, summer's great. Smell the woods?" She began whistling a tune, trilling sweet as bird-song.

At half past ten she stopped the truck in front of a small garage in the village of St. Paul.

"Be hot enough to fry in there today. Oh well, if we get at it we'll be on our way home by three." She hopped out of the truck, heaved the heavy tool sack out of the box, and headed for the garage.

André, feeling piqued and a bit foolish, tagged after her.

Had her figured for a hot one, and after all the come-on she's been giving me hanging around Mason's, she ain't even —

Dolores was talking to the proprietor when André entered the garage. The car they were to work on was already set up under the hoist.

"You right-handed, André?" Dolores asked.

"Yeah."

"I'm left. So you work on this side, and I'll work on the other."

She had the hood open and was lining up her tools before André moved. Mason's brother was watching with a sardonic grin on his face. André headed for the car, adding to his embarrassment by stumbling over a wrench lying on the cement floor.

Damn her! Sailing in here like she's a master mechanic, and I'll bet she's as useless as the tits on a bull.

But in fifteen minutes he was grudgingly admitting that Dolores knew as much about cars as he did.

Jeez! Look at her. Grease to the armpits and sweating like a pig. I gotta get my ass in gear —

When the fire-hall siren blew at noon, Dolores backed off from the car, rubbing her forearm over her dripping brow. "Whew! We're going great. Another couple of hours, and we'll have her licked. Wanna go eat?"

"Bill said to buy us a good lunch," he said, fishing the twenty out of the watch pocket of his jeans.

"Oh, Mom packed our dinner, and there's a neat little park we passed back there."

He shrugged, refolded the money, and thrust it as deep as it would go into his pocket. Dolores watched him speculatively, one grease-blackened finger toying absently with a small pimple beside her nose.

The breeze was sweet under the dappling tree shadows in the park. They ate thick roast beef sandwiches hot with mustard and gooseberry tarts for dessert. While they rested André amused himself by enticing a chipmunk close enough to take the leftover bread crusts.

"Sure hate to go back in that garage right now," he said. "Thunderstorm's building. Be cooler after it rains."

"Nothing doing. Let's get at it." She looked at him through her eyelashes. "Remember the lake we passed on the way down? Wouldn't a swim be super after the day we've put in?" She giggled and poked him in the ribs.

He was instantly — and alarmingly — horny. "Hey! A swim. That's great."

Task completed, they were whistling north along the highway. The day was murky and oppressive. Not a breath of air moved. Sweat burned and pricked at the back of André's knees, and his shirt was plastered to the seat back. He watched the thunder cloud gathering itself in the west.

"Gonna be a dandy when she hits."

"Hope so. Nothing like a lightning storm. Mom takes Astrid and hides in the cellar, but I wish it'd go on all night. Burn the barn, or the house, or—" She interrupted herself with laughter. "Or even me!"

They came suddenly upon the lake, a dull mirror in the heat, with mud hens drowsing in the reeds. Dolores braked and eased the truck down a sandy side road and into a heavy growth of willows where it would be hidden from the highway. She shut off the engine and stretched, arms overhead, wrists grasped. André could almost feel the tension of her singing muscles transferred to him through the fabric of the seat. She grinned at him and sprang from the truck.

"Last one in's a rotten egg!" She slammed the truck door and sprinted for the water, shedding clothes as she ran. Before André was out of the truck she hit the water with a great "Waa-hooo!" of joy.

Man! She's a crazy broad!

The water was sweet to his heat-prickled, sweaty skin. He launched himself strongly toward the centre of the lake, turning somersaults. He dived and surfaced with a stone clutched triumphantly in his fist before he realized he was swimming alone. Treading water, he turned to look back. Dolores was standing waist-deep, looking after him.

"Thought you wanted a swim."

Her voice, child-like and undulating, came to him over the distance. "I never learned how."

Well, I sure as hell *did*, and this is the first chance I've had all summer.

After fifteen minutes in the deep water when he turned for shore, expecting Dolores' adulation for his prowess, he was surprised to see her standing fully dressed on the beach.

"Hey! Don't you wanna lay in the sand, an'—"

"Hurry up. We gotta get outta here."

"Huh?"

"Couple of kids sneaking through the bush."

"So what?"

"If Daddy found out I was skinny dippin' with a guy, he'd kill me."

"You know the kids?"

"Never seen 'em real close, but we better get outta here. Get your clothes on."

He grimaced in chagrin. Blew it! She was all set for a little nooky. Lost her nerve while I was out horsing around in the lake. There's no kids. She's just — Jeez! I'm a dumb ass!

On the way home Dolores pushed the old truck to its capacity. André watched the thunder cloud build itself and made no attempt to talk to her. When she let him out in front of Mason's garage it was almost quitting time. She glanced at him before she drove off, a guarded expression on her face, and no hint of coquettishness.

Forget about that piece of tail, he thought sourly.

Mason was checking out the till when André walked in. "Hey, André, change from that twenty — ?"

"Never had to break it." He dug his finger into his watch pocket. "What the hell? It's gone. Jeez! I had it at noon — "

Mason scowled. "Never heard of a guy losing money out of a watch pocket."

"Neither did — "

Dolores! Musta pinched it while I was in the lake. The bitch! Made up a couple of kids —

"You better go through your other pockets," Mason said.

After André had done so he scowled at his boots and shrugged. "Well — If you wanna nick my wages — "

"I'm sure as hell gonna nick your wages. Jesus! Money don't grow on trees."

André stalked out of the garage as the town was hit by the first rushing gust of wind preceding the thunder storm. A gash of green lightning and a simultaneous crash of thunder threw his heart into his mouth. He began to run. Rain slashed his head and shoulders. He was still three blocks from home when wind-driven hail added to the rain forced him to dive across the road and take refuge in an abandoned chicken coop. He crouched, shivering in the doorway, nose assaulted by the stench of wet chicken shit, and watched the storm.

He had seldom seen such lightning. It hissed and sizzled around him. The earth shuddered with thunder.

She wanted lightning. Hope it burns her ass.

Suddenly he giggled.

Cost me twenty bucks, but I learned something. Never leave my pants where a broad can get her fist into the pocket.

Or did she? Maybe there *was* kids sneaking through the bush.

Ah! To hell with it. Tonight I'm gonna see Dodie.

five

For the next three days André's relationship with Bill Mason was decidedly cool, but the weather remained hot. Miserably so. One steaming afternoon Mason scrunched down on the mechanic's creeper beside Dr. Pêche's Citroen with the huge orange manual in his hands and a puzzled scowl on his face.

"Jesus! I'm dripping," he said for the fourth time in ten minutes. With the back of his hand he wiped at sweat trickling down his forehead, smearing himself with black grease. He held the manual out at arm's length and squinted at it. "Damn fancy foreign cars!" he exploded. "Me with a pair of busted glasses—" He thrust the manual at André. "Read that part about bleeding the hydraulic system in this fool thing, willya?"

André read the passage, then read it aloud, bit by bit, at the same time using his finger as a pointer in the workings of the car. Mason pulled at his chin and glowered, then his face brightened and he grinned. "Got it. Sure as hell!" He looked at André appraisingly. "Ever think of studying mechanics?"

"Nah." He took some pebbles he had picked up on his way to work that morning and turned them over and over in his hands.

"How come you always got a pocketful of rocks?"

André shrugged, went to the garage door and pitched the stones into the willow scrub in the vacant lot next door.

Rocks in my head! Boxes of 'em in the rafters and I can classify 'em forty different ways. Big deal.

He slouched against the doorway in the still, hot air. One of the tiny, vicious mosquitoes of late summer attacked the back of his hand. He watched it swell with blood and finally fly off, so bloated it could scarcely keep aloft.

An ancient Volkswagen plastered with flower decals pulled in beside the gas pumps. Dave Crumley stuck his red head out of the window and shouted, "How'd you make out, Brains?"

Brains! Goddamn him. Hope Mason never heard that.

"Make out?"

"Grade twelve results are in the mail. Didn't you hear?"

Unease stirred in André's stomach. He deliberately changed the subject. "Whaddya been doin' all summer?"

"Oh—Getting lined up for university." He put the car in gear.

"Well, just curious to see how my math and chem marks lined up with yours—"

"Wanna run me down to the post office? Mason'd give me ten minutes."

Crumley's face coloured. "Well—tell you the truth, I'm in kind of a rush, but if I see Father Pépin—"

Stuck up sonofabitch! And *that* old buzzard'll be on my back soon enough.

"Didn't I hear something about you going to technical school?" Crumley probed.

"Not from me, you never."

"What are you gonna do?"

"Dunno. Maybe just be a bum."

Crumley grinned at him, let out the clutch and chugged out of the lot.

If I knew the goddamn marks were lousy, I wouldn't have to do nothing, André thought sourly.

All that afternoon he hung about the garage making odd jobs for himself. It was a dead day. Not half a dozen customers came in. Finally he loaded the truck with empty oil cans and drove out to the town dump. It reeked of decay in the heat. Gulls quarrelled over mouldy bread crusts and blue-bottle flies buzzed frantically over the rotting body of a small animal. When André had pitched the last can out of the truck box he thankfully climbed into the cab. As he was turning the key in the ignition, two grinning, brown faces appeared at the window.

"Hey! Alphonse—Willie. Ain't seen you guys since—"

"You gettin' things ass-backwards these days, André," Alphonse said mockingly.

"Yeah! Jeez!" Willie took it up. "Us breeds takes junk *outta* du dump. Don't bring junk *into* it." He leaned his forearms on

26

the window of the truck, grinning appreciatively at André's chuckles.

"How 'bout runnin' us down to Loon Point?" Alphonse asked. "Got du fish nets set out — "

"And dere's Angie Snowbird and Bessie Yellow Shoes waitin' for us down dat place," Willie added. "Man, all dey need is a slug of beer — "

"We got du beer," Alphonse chortled, "but du Ford quit on us. Goin' fine, but we went off in du bush to take a leak, and du bugger won't start now." He opened the truck door and confidently climbed in beside André, Willie following.

"Loon Point? Take a couple of hours. Mason'd have the Mountie chasin' me."

"Shit! After a couple of beers, who cares?"

"Jeez, guys, there's no way. But grab that old pail. Might get the Ford goin'. Sounds like a vapour lock."

Alphonse and Willie fell silent, their faces suddenly closed and sullen. They watched like two sick birds, the beaks of their caps turned up, shoulders hunched, fists deep in pants pockets, while André doused the engine of the Ford with ditch water. When he tried the engine it sputtered into life.

"Guess the white man don't drink beer with us dirty breeds no more, huh?" Alphonse threw over his shoulder at André as he and Willie drove off.

"Jesus shittin' Christ!" André gritted, kicking savagely at clumps of dirt along the ditch bank. Automatically, he picked up several dislodged pebbles, stared at them, and dropped them into his pocket.

Father Pépin was waiting for him in the shade of the garage. "André! Hurry before the post office closes. Mr. Mason gives you permission — "

Oh, Christ! Here it comes —

Half an hour later he was sitting across the desk from Father Pépin in the austere rectory study. The old priest sat with his neck sticking out like a newly-wakened chicken's; his black eyes were gimlets of concentration as he pored over the Department of Education transcript of André's high school marks.

"Best marks are in the sciences. Could be successful in any one of perhaps — umm, four fields." He tossed the transcript on the desk and threw himself back in the chair. "Two things I 'ave waited for. One is this." He pointed at the paper. "Although, of course, I knew—The other, perhaps more important, I wished to make certain that you could 'old a job. So many Métis cannot, or will not. Mason tells me you are a dependable worker, so—" He paused portentously.

Sweat burst out on the palms of André's hands.

"So . . . what are you going to study?"

"Might be a stupid breed, but I know five hundred dollars I'll earn this summer don't—"

"Ach! Since I saw your grade *nine* results, I 'ave marked you. Any discipline you wish to pursue, I 'ave the money for it."

Blood hissed in André's ears, and his toes scrunched in his shoes. He could not look at Father Pépin.

"Well?"

He shook his head mutely, eyes clinging to a glass paper-weight on the desk. The painful moment swelled and swelled.

"You know 'ow long I 'ave been with your people? Forty-two years. And in all that time, *one* of you I get through 'igh school. *One.* My brother priests say it cannot be done. It 'as been done."

"Yeah, Father, it's been done. And where does it leave me? I'm the guy that's good enough to help the bigshot lawyer's kid with his chemistry experiments, but I ain't good enough to ride in his car. His Ma might see him, ask what he's doing chasin' around with that goddamn breed—I'm the guy that ain't got brains enough to go with Willie and Alphonse this afternoon, and to hell with Mason's truck. 'Guess the white man don't drink beer with us dirty breeds no more' Alphonse says. So where am I? Shit outta luck, don't matter where I turn."

"André, this little place, this village — It is nothing," the priest's voice was soft and insinuating. "There will come a day when you can take your place with the best-educated white men in this country, if you will—"

"Be a white fella? That's good? You wanna say to them priests you're talkin' about, 'Look! I made a white man outta this stupid sonofabitch.' Only I ain't a white man, ever. Like in school — They never threw rocks at me, but they never said, 'Hey, André, come over to my place.' Mostly, I just ain't *there.* Not unless somebody needs to get the answer to a math problem or something. You wanna stick me in some other kinda jail where they ram my head fulla crap, but *I* — me — I'm zero!"

The priest reared to his feet, his wrinkled hands knuckled and white on top of the oaken desk. "Jail, you say to me? Lonely, you say? All my life I am lonely. For you, and others like you. I lay the world at your feet, and you spit on it!" He rounded the desk and stood over André. "Don't bleat to me that you are lonely. You owe *me* something. Be lonely in order to become. I'll not let you off from it. Too many years of prayer and 'ard work 'ave gone into you."

He swung away, yanked open the top drawer of his desk, swooped two slender booklets out of it and threw them at André. "Read them. And when you come to your senses, talk to me again."

André sat in the middle of Cy Grossman's oat field for a long time, alternately shaking and cursing.

Old bastard never gives up. Calendars for the University of Alberta, and the Northern Alberta Institute of Technology. Shit!

Suddenly he began to laugh, a wrenching laughter that left his eyes wet with tears.

Jesus, I dunno—Do I owe him something? Maybe it is stupid to holler about being lonely. Who ain't? Maybe it's even stupid to be scared of going to Edmonton. It's just a place. People learn to live there.

He picked up the two calendars and slowly waded through the field of hip-high oats. In the shade of a dense spruce thicket, he dropped down in the shade and listened to the stillness. The air was sweet with the clean tang of hot spruce gum. The song of a whitethroat penetrated the afternoon. Chokecherries ripened in the bush at the edge of the oat field, and back in the woods quaking aspen leaves shivered in the hot, motionless air.

It's the bush. I dunno how in Christ I'll ever learn to live without the bush.

There was no one in the shack when he got home. The door was wide open. He remembered Rachel saying that they were all going to pick blueberries.

André flung himself belly down on the bed. With a sigh, he opened the calendar for the Northern Alberta Institute of Technology. He thumbed through it, found the Earth Resources program again and re-read it.

Two years—Jeez! I wonder—? End up with a job for a mining

company, maybe. Or like that seismic crew that's out there in the bush—Might not be so bad. Wouldn't be cooped up in some kinda office all the time. Not once I finished the course—

The rocks in his thigh pocket were digging uncomfortably into his leg. He fished them out and laid them on top of the calendar.

Nothing much here—Schist. Must be a lot of that over where Chickadee got that sand. Garnets occur in it sometimes. This—nothing. Chunk of shale.

He gave the shale a sharp tap on the iron bed frame. It split laterally, exposing a perfect trilobite fossil.

"Jesus!" He sprang from the bed staring at his find.

"What're you doing, André?" Dodie Rose was standing in the doorway.

"Look at this. Cambrian trilobite! He was crawlin' around when this country was an ocean, five hundred million years ago."

"Oh, for godsake, what are you tryin' to give me? When this country was an ocean!"

"Look at him though."

"Nuts! A bug's still a bug. What're you doin' home early?"

She was wearing a bikini of a brilliant orange and blue flowered material. At the sight of her André felt his groin grow heavy and hot. He grabbed her. "Couldn't wait—"

She squirmed away from him. "Jesus! Can't you think of anythin' else? I'm so hot I'm cookin', even in *this*, and you wanna—"

"Thought you was wearin' that so I'd wanna."

She swept her long blonde hair back with a gesture which reminded him of a cat that has had its fur mussed, and slapped at a mosquito on her thigh. "Damn mosquitoes! Damn hot weather! Kid's been bawlin' all day. Finally played out ten minutes ago."

She wandered about the shack, looked with distaste at the table with its load of unwashed dishes and repeated. "So hot I'm cookin', and these bloody mosquitoes—" She slapped at the side of her neck.

"How come white people always belly-ache 'bout flies, or mosquitoes? And weather—You can't do nothin' about it."

"You can put up screens to keep the bugs out. Albert done that much. Why don't you come over to my place for a beer?"

She spotted the two academic calendars lying on the bed, picked them up and peered at them.

"What's this stuff?"

"Might be goin' for that Earth Resources course."

"You're kiddin'!" There was disbelief and amazement in her voice.

Stung, André took the envelope containing the transcript of his marks and tossed it across to her. She cast him a sidelong glance, picked up the paper from the floor where it had fallen, and read down the list, lips moving. She laid the paper on the table. Her expression was both sly and vaguely spiteful.

"Well—What do you know?" She giggled. "I graduated early."

"Yeah?"

"Yeah. English teacher caught me and a guy out in the parkin' lot — Fuckin' in the back seat of a car."

"Sister Bridget catch anybody doin' that and she'd die of a shit hemorrhage."

They laughed uncontrollably.

Dodie wiped her eyes on the back of her hand. "School — Christ!" she said contemptuously. "C'mon, let's go. These mosquitoes are eatin' the ass offa me."

Just off the edge of the stoop, she stopped and turned to him. "You're not serious about that . . . what is it, technical school or somethin'?"

"Dunno. Father Pépin says — "

"Father Pépin!" she snorted. "Dumb old turd! Whaddya wanna leave for? You got a job, and I'm gonna be around a while. Albert's got a contract, kinda. It'll last till after Christmas. Road construction south of Edmonton. Don't see him drivin' three hundred miles to get home many Saturday nights."

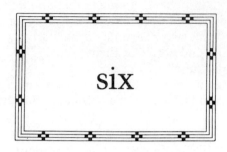

six

For two weeks André lived in a state swinging between euphoria and despair. There was work every day, Dodie every night, and long hours spent hesitating through academic calendars. Time and again he could not summon the will to go to Father Pépin with a firm decision.

One Sunday morning he slipped cautiously out of Dodie's bed. He didn't want to waken her. She teased him unmercifully about going to Mass. As he reached for his pants, she grabbed him around the neck and sank her sharp little teeth into the skin at his waist.

"Ummm! Good," she said pulling him over on top of her. "Now where dya think you're goin'?"

"Quit it, Dodie. I gotta — "

"You gotta, have you?"

"C'mon, leggo."

"Uh-uh! You come back here. There's somethin' you gotta do first."

"Aw, c'mon!" he said, jerking her arm away from his neck.

She giggled. "Can't get it up this morning, huh?"

Anger stirred in him. "Well, jeez! Enough is enough."

She laughed outright. "Aw! Is 'im ty-ed? Du poor baby — " It was a mock croon.

"Shut up, goddamn it! I'm sick of hearin' you — "

"*You're* sick of hearin' *me*!" She snapped to a sitting position.

"Well, goddamn you. I'm sick of feedin' you, and fuckin' you, and listenin' to you babble about geology, and biology, and — whatever-the-hell it is."

"Yeah! Geology or biology, or *whatever-the-hell it is!* You wouldn't know. You're so dumb you can't add up your store bill and get it right."

She sprang from the bed, snatched up the two calendars which were lying on the table and threw them at him. She pointed angrily. "Take that crap and get out! *Breed!* Just like all the rest of 'em—Gonna do wonders and shit cucumbers, and you'll end up on welfare wipin' your ass on pages out of the Eaton's catalogue."

André yanked on his clothes, snatched up the calendars and slammed out of the house. He was about to plunge into the bush on the other side of the road, but it was an overcast, chilly morning. The trees were dripping from rain. Fall was in the air. He could not face the prospect of going into his father's shack, and Mass was out of the question. He turned toward the centre of town. The hotel coffee shop would be open.

The café was warm and smelled richly of fresh coffee, toast, and frying bacon. Genevieve Dupée, the proprietor's daughter, was working behind the counter. André and she had known each other since grade one. She glanced up at him, smiled, and said with casual friendliness, "Hi, André. Not going to Mass this morning?"

"Guess not."

"Me neither. Got the morning shift. What'll you have?"

"Coffee. Toast and jam, maybe."

"Coming up as soon as I finish this order." She ran a cup of coffee out of the urn and set it in front of him. "Hold you a minute?"

"Yeah. Thanks." He poured three huge spoonfuls of sugar into the mug and laced it with cream, then sat staring at it. He was still queasy with rage.

Stupid bitch of a Dodie! How long am I gonna stand for her calling me a breed? Poking fun at me—Making out like I'm too dumb to—Well, not smart—Fooling with her, 'cause if Albert caught up to me—Jeez! Suppose she gets spiteful? He gulped the coffee. It hit the bottom of his stomach. He wondered if it was going to stay down.

Genevieve was serving bacon and pancakes to the seismic crew who boarded at the hotel. They chattered among themselves, teased her, and exploded in great guffaws of comfortable laughter.

André's mouth watered at the smell of bacon.

Lucky bastards. Good clothes, full bellies, and fancy cars. Bet some of 'em got some pretty fancy women, too. Nice. Like—Well, Genevieve.

Always been decent to me. In church, or in school. Wonder what'd happen if—Don't be stupid! Old man Dupée and the old woman don't let their daughter go with breeds.

But I ain't a bad looking guy. He examined himself in the mirror he faced across the counter. Heard 'em say I could pass for a dark white fella. Good teeth. Hell, quit kidding yourself! Whadda you think teeth got to do with it?

He took the two academic calendars out of the pocket of his parka, spread them on the counter and began to read them again.

Wish I *knew* more about this stuff, but I gotta make up my mind. Father's gonna give me shit tomorrow night—

He was concentrating so deeply that he started when Genevieve brought his toast.

"André! A University calendar. Wow! Father Pépin was telling me how well you'd done in the departmentals."

"How about you?"

"Not bad. I've been accepted for nurses' training at the University of Alberta hospital."

Nurse — and Crumley going into medicine. Me with more brains than either of 'em, and here I sit picking my nose and balling Dodie Rose. If I don't make up my goddamn mind I'll be doing just what Dodie said, living on welfare and wiping my ass on the Eaton's catalogue.

"So, what are you going into, André?"

"Geology. Earth Resources. Northern Alberta Institute of Technology, y'know?"

Did I say that? Me? Jeez!

"Sounds right." Genevieve cocked her dark hair to one side as she considered. "I learned a lot about rocks and minerals from that report you did back in grade nine." She laughed. "Do you still carry rocks in your pocket?"

André laughed with her. He was suddenly expansive and at ease as he fetched the latest find out to show her.

"Got somethin' kinda interestin' here." He handed her a small stone. "Notice anythin' funny about that?"

She turned it in her hands doubtfully. "Well — Round?"

He handed her another of equal size to compare. She weighed them, one in each hand. "Good grief! First one's heavy."

"And rust brown. Lot of iron ore, I figure."

"Neat! Now to me, that's just another little old rock."

She carried the two stones across to where the seismic crew were still drinking coffee, and handed them to a slim-faced fellow of about thirty.

He examined the rusty stone intently. "Where'd you get this?"

She gestured toward André. "*He* found it. André, come and meet Bob Thompson. André wants to go into geology too, Bob."

"Geology, huh?" Thompson grinned at André and indicated an empty chair. "Wanna coffee?"

Thompson talked to him long after the other members of the seismic crew had wandered off.

"You sure told me a lot of stuff," André said gratefully, after the third cup of coffee. "That course don't seem so scary now."

"Nice to know what you're getting into."

"I — I never been out of the bush, though."

"Nothing to it. I'd hardly been off the farm in Saskatchewan before I went to university."

André thanked him for the coffee and left the café. He started purposefully up the hill toward the rectory as brilliant sunshine broke through the rain clouds.

Going right up there and tell Father.

Then his steps faltered, and he stopped.

Nothing to it, huh? Damn near had me fooled there for a minute. Forgot. He's a white guy. I'm a breed.

He retraced his steps, crossed the road, and walked out onto the wharf that projected into the lake. The Sunday morning fishermen had departed, and the place was deserted, save for the gulls and two ancient boats rotting on the beach. He perched on the wharf, legs dangling, eyes narrowed against the shining lake. For a long time he stared down into the black water beside the pilings.

"Oh, hell, it's no use," he sighed at last. "I gotta get it over with."

It was a frantically busy week. Every time he turned around it seemed that Father Pépin stood at his elbow with papers for him to sign, or reports of phone calls to Edmonton making arrangements on his behalf.

"You are fortunate," the priest told him. "The Earth Resources program was full, but three students dropped out. It is only because I am a good talker, and your 'igh school marks are as good as they are that they are allowing you in." He rubbed his hands together, a grin of satisfaction on his face. "'owever, it is done. I 'ave found a boarding place for you in the city. It sounds ideal. The woman 'erself is Métis. They are not Catholic, but I am assured they are good people. You 'ave a week until the end of August. Then I will take you to Edmonton myself and see you settled." He clapped André on the shoulder. "You are 'appy?"

"I dunno, Father," André gulped. "Maybe just — scared."

"Don't be! There is a good life waiting for you."

Hope he knows what he's talking about, André thought as he plodded toward home that night. Right now I feel as if I was driving down the hill to the Heintzberg ferry with the brakes failing.

As he approached Isaac's shack he saw Dodie Rose standing in the couch grass across the fence, hanging diapers on her sagging clothesline. She ignored him. Except for a small hint of agitation in her movements he might have thought she hadn't seen him.

So she ain't talking. Suits me fine. Got enough woman trouble these days with Ma without *her*.

"You gotta wear what you're standin' up in next week," Chickadee told him as he entered the shack. "Ma and me got all your clothes in this box. Clean. I even darned your socks."

"Makes two more fools in dis house besides you," Rachel grunted. She squatted on a backless kitchen chair, a can of Macdonald's fine cut tobacco clamped between her knees as she rolled a cigarette. "Goin' to du city, for a breed is du same as goin' to hell. Dat Gary One Blanket—Laura Picard—Simone—" She turned on Isaac who was sharpening a jack-knife on a whet stone cupped in his palm. "Kid's leavin' home to study *rocks*, and you don't say nothin'?"

Isaac examined André with a sullen, sidelong glance, shrugged, spat on the stone and went on grinding the knife.

"All I know, they're sayin' after I finish this course I can get a job with an oil company, or a minin' outfit," André muttered.

"Yeah! Cleaning dere shit houses, might be!"

36

Isaac stopped grinding his knife. He sat very still, head cocked to one side as though he were listening. "Gonna snow," he muttered. "Seven days. Might be eight — "

"Seven, eight days?" André said, relieved at the chance to change the subject. "Be the day of the rodeo. Mason'll sure be sore if he don't get to drive his Tin Lizzie in the parade."

"Gonna snow," Isaac repeated and tested the knife for sharpness on the edge of the plastic table cloth.

Rachel got up and went to the stove. She opened the oven and stuck one hand in to test the heat, threw several more chunks of wood into the fire-box, then shoved four loaves of bread into the oven.

"Rocks. Shit!" she muttered. She rounded on André. "You wanna study rocks? Open du door. Rocks every goddamn place you look."

seven

It was the day of the town's annual fair and rodeo, the last day of August, and André's last day at the garage. He hurried along the lakeshore road that morning through the warm sunshine admiring the odd coin dot of gold in the poplar leaves.

Old man's still saying it's gonna snow. He grinned. Got his wires crossed.

Mason met André at the door of the garage. He was decked out in a 1917 outfit, complete with gauntlets and goggles. "I'm taking the morning off," he announced. "All you gotta do is pump gas and change the odd tire. Fan belts, stuff like that. I'm paying you time and a half, so you got nothing to squawk about."

He rushed into the garage and fired up the Tin Lizzie. Then childish with excitement, he chugged out to find his place in the parade.

André stood in the open doorway watching two cowboys taking the kinks out of their roping horses in the middle of Main Street. Alphonse, Willie, and two girls slouched by on the far side of the street without seeming to notice him. Gangs of small boys, each one trying to out-yell his fellows, rushed hither and thither. Simone sauntered past, with Joey tagging behind her. The little boy seemed to have a bad cold. He coughed, and wiped his nose on his shirt sleeve.

Damn job! André thought. Wonder what Mason'd say if I locked the joint and took off to the rodeo? Jeez! I sure wanna, but — he sighed.

It was a frantically busy morning. Cars, sometimes four at a time, lined up at the gas pumps, forcing André to move at a steady shambling trot. During one flurry of patronage, he was startled by a girl rolling down the window of a car waiting in the line-up and emitting an ear-piercing wolf-whistle. Dolores Olson hung out of the car window grinning at him, green eyes a-glint.

"Hey, André," she shouted, "taken the engines out of any cars lately?"

The car's driver, who André knew must be her brother, the teacher, turned and spoke sharply to her. The woman on the seat beside him ducked her head, shadowing her eyes with her hand, her face flaming. Dolores pulled herself back into the car, but when it stopped at the gas pumps she flicked André a glance and grinned provocatively, jaws moving over a wad of gum.

All cleaned up and wearing a dress. Wonder where she's going?

Dolores' brother got out of the car to watch the gassing up. His wife slipped into the driver's seat and called out to him: "Oh, Thorvald, the windshield wipers — Remember?"

"Yeah. Forecast's for rain or snow this afternoon," he told André. "Blades on my wipers are shot. Got anything that'll fit?"

"Nothin' for this model. But I can fix you somethin' that'll work if you wanna wait till I'm through with these guys behind you."

"Yeah. Be okay. Anyhow, I want to take a look at that Model T Mason fixed up. Dad was talking about it."

"Seen Mason drivin' it down to his place ten minutes ago."

"Just a block down. Want to come, Sandra?"

"Honey, I'm not interested in old cars," the woman answered in a carefully modulated voice. "Dolores and I will wait. Don't be too long. I have an appointment in Edmonton at four o'clock to have something done to her hair." As Thorvald sauntered away, she expertly backed the car up beside the garage door out of the way of the gas pumps.

André finished with the gas sales and began adapting the new wiper blades to fit the car.

"Dunno what you and Thorvald got so sore about, Sandra," he overheard Dolores say.

"Dolores, nice girls don't wolf-whistle and shout at fellows. You want to be a secretary. There's more to it than learning to type and take shorthand. Good offices hire girls who know how to behave properly. That gum, for instance. A habit like that could get you fired."

"Oh, *brother!*" Dolores muttered resentfully.

"Now, look, Thorvald and I are taking you into our home and paying for a secretarial course for you. The least you can do—"

Dolores better watch her step with that broad, André thought. First time she lifts a buck out of her pocket—Oh, screw it! I don't *know* she took that twenty.

When the car drove off after Thorvald had returned, Dolores looked back at André. Her fingers moved in a subdued, hopeful wave. He grinned and waved back.

Wonder if I'll run into her in Edmonton? Ain't likely.

Mason appeared, dressed in working clothes. He reeked of beer, but he was not drunk, only happy, and slightly uninhibited.

"Sure as hell gonna miss you around here," he told André. "You've turned into a pretty good pump jockey, and I notice if you fix something it stays fixed. Now, if you was to study automotives instead of geology—Hell, there's a job for you right here."

"Don't like the stink of grease but thanks, that's — yeah, thanks."

In the late afternoon the weather shifted with unnerving abruptness. Wind straight off the Polar Ice Cap slammed down the Mackenzie Trough and hit the town like a dash of icewater in the face. The rodeo disintegrated. Cars and trucks laden with shivering families in shirtsleeves and summer dresses clogged the streets of the town. Business had been brisk before the storm hit; it became frantic afterwards. André had worked in rolled up shirtsleeves that morning. Now he scuttled about, back to the wind, eyes narrowed against it and his bush shirt buttoned to the neck.

"Gonna snow, sure as you're born," Mason predicted as he lit the propane heater in the gas station office.

A gravel truck, box jouncing, slammed to a stop in front of the gas pumps. Steeling himself against the wind, André trotted out and around to the driver's side.

Albert Rose! His heart quickened. But if Rose recognized him, he gave no sign. "Fill 'er up," he grunted. Squinting against the wind, he got out of the cab to check tire pressure and oil level himself. André couldn't keep his eyes away from the man's massive shoulders and thick-fingered hands.

Rose, seeming to sense André's eyes upon him, turned and

scowled from where he crouched beside one of the rear wheels. "What's the hold up? Get that windshield cleaned, inside and out."

Wet chamois in hand, André climbed into the cab of the truck. It reeked of stale sweat and cigarette smoke. As he rubbed at the inside of the murky windshield he glanced into the side mirror. A string of cars with impatient drivers were lined up waiting a turn at the pumps. Rose removed the gas hose himself and slammed into the truck. André slid across the seat, grasped the door handle and twisted. It would not turn. He felt trapped. His heart slammed painfully.

"Sit tight," Rose growled. "Handle's busted. I'll just pull out of the way so these sonsabitches behind me can—" After three tries the motor sputtered and fired. Rose glowered at the gauges. "Fuckin' generator! Battery ain't chargin'." He slammed the truck into gear and let out the clutch.

Oh, Jesus, he's got me! *He knows!* He's gonna get me off by myself and—

Rose drove out of the service station lot and parked on the shoulder of the muddy road. He turned on André and demanded, "Mason busy tonight?"

"Huh?" André croaked.

"What the hell's wrong with you? I said, *is Mason busy tonight?*"

"Mason—? Oh, no. Nothin' in the shop. Just the gas pumps."

"Well, he's gonna be, like it or not, and I'm keepin' an eye on the old bugger. Ain't paying him to sit around scratchin' his ass." He wrenched the door open and climbed down. Suppressed violence was in his every move and in every snap of his speech.

André slid across the seat, under the wheel and past Rose. His knees quivered unsteadily when he landed on the ground. He sprinted for the service station.

Figured I'd had it. Bastard had me cornered. God! What if— But who's gonna blab? Not Ma, or the old man. Not Dodie. He'd beat the shit outta her, too. And next week *I'm* gone."

At closing time Mason, working under Rose's baleful eye, looked up from the workbench where he was engaged in the tedious task of rewinding the generator coil of the truck. "Take what's comin' to you outta the till, willya, André? And—Well, be seein' ya before ya take off for Edmonton."

Don't wanna carry that much money around in my pocket, and Father Pépin's away at a funeral in Grande Prairie. Should ask Bill to keep it till — Shit! Think I was three years old.

As he closed the till Rose moved toward him and ordered, "Tell Dodie I'll be home a little after eight. Want steak for supper, and lots of it."

Jeez! Dodie — But if I say I ain't gonna do it, it's gonna look funny.

"Yeah, okay," he muttered as he went out into the night. He ducked his face into the rain-slashed wind salted with snowflakes and hurried toward home.

Dodie, cigarette in hand, opened the door to his knock. "Whadda you want?"

André delivered Rose's message.

"Steak? The sonofabitch! What does he expect me to do? Go kill a cow? Never leaves enough money. Fairfax cut me off groceries."

Lying bitch. I seen her sporting a new coat and one of them fancy pant suits. And beer —

"Yeah. Well — " He moved off the step. "Guess I'll — "

"André, come in a minute." She caught him by the sleeve of his wet bush shirt; reluctantly, he allowed himself to be pulled into the house. She shut the door in the face of the wind and leaned against it, hands behind her back, as though to bar his escape.

"You get paid tonight?"

"Yeah."

"Well, look, lemme have some money, willya? I'm in a hell of a spot. Albert finds out I got no groceries in the house, and he's gonna — "

With a sinking sensation in the pit of his stomach, he extracted the roll of bills from his pocket, peeled off a ten and handed it to her.

"Ten lousy dollars? What'll *that* buy? I need at least fifty."

"Fifty? Jesus!"

She held out her hand. "Gimme, gimme, gimme."

"Dodie!"

"Leave me in a jam like this and I'll fix you good." Her tone was savage. "You guzzled fifty dollars' worth of steaks and beer around here this summer. You owe me — "

"Huh! Who owes who? Good question!" He was suddenly recklessly angry. "Maybe it's *you* that oughtta be payin' me."

She sprang at him, painted nails raking his face before he could raise a hand to protect himself. He grabbed her wrists and slammed her against the door. With a twist of his thigh he blocked the knee she aimed at his groin. He yanked her away from the door and flung her across the room to land sprawling on the bed, then fled the house, leaving the door open to the wind.

"You wait, you bastard! You just wait!" her voice screamed after him through the night.

André burst through the door into the dark shack.

Nobody home.

"André?"

"What're you doin' alone here in the dark, Joey?"

"Sick. So — so cold."

André fumbled around in the shelves until he found the box of matches. He lit the kerosene lamp with a quivering hand. It was cold in the shack; the stove must have gone out hours ago.

Joey was a small sad heap under the dirty blankets and the additional cover of two old parkas. His face was greyish yellow; his eyes dull black beads that refused to focus.

"Where's Ma?"

The child did not answer.

"Joey?"

He stirred and muttered something André could not understand.

Christ! Where's Ma? Well — Saturday night. I know *where.* And Simone. Chicky went to Bonnyville with Max and the old lady after the stampede.

"Cold," Joey quavered.

André lifted the lid from the kitchen range. Wind puffed down the chimney, sifting the cold, grey ashes. There was no wood in the box, and no kindling cut.

André went out into the wind to find the axe against the chopping block. Now the sleet was giving way to heavy gobs of wet snow. He selected a chunk of seasoned, straight-grained pine, and took it and the axe into the house where he slivered the wood into kindling. Then he went out for several armfuls of logs.

Wet wood. Have a hell of a time starting that fire.

As he hurried in with his fourth load, he scowled at the propane tank standing outside Rose's house.

Too bad that bitch didn't have to cut wood to keep warm. Maybe then she wouldn't have time for —

He blundered into Joey standing bare-footed on the snow-covered step.

"The weetigo! The weetigo!"

"Joey, get back in bed. There's no old woman gonna eat you."

The child ignored him and, weaving drunkenly, made off into the dark. André tossed his load of wood against the stove and rushed after him, picked him up, carried him back inside to the bed, and heaped the covers on top of him.

"Now, you stay there!"

Kid's out of his head, he thought, as he set a match to the kindling. If somebody don't stop him he'll head off into the dark. What the hell am I gonna do? Gotta be out of here before Rose gets home. That damn Dodie — She'll say I tried to rape her. He'll be over here to stomp the guts out of me. But I can't leave the kid. Not a light on in any of the shacks around. They're all at the stampede dance. If Chicky'd show up I could send her for Ma — She might come pretty soon.

The hope sustained him while the fire roared in the chimney and the shack began to warm. But by half-past seven he was desperate. The night outside had turned unto a minor blizzard. Joey rolled, and tossed, and muttered. Twice he got out of bed, screaming at some terror in his delirium. He was burning hot to the touch, yet he shivered like an aspen leaf when André carried him back to bed and covered him again.

Can't leave him. Jeez! If somebody'd come—But they won't. All I can do is barricade the door and that one window where a guy could climb through. Blow out the lamp. Pretend nobody's here.

He forced three knives into the door framework and jammed a chair under the knob, then upended Isaac and Rachel's bed and stomped the spring out of the bedstead. He dragged the spring across to the bigger of the two windows and braced it there with a couple of benches, then puffed out the light.

Joey screamed.

"Shut up, kid! Shut up!" André hissed.

The child subsided into whimpers. André sat on the bed beside him, hushing him from time to time.

The wind, now approaching gale force, wailed through a crack in the tar paper. A tree branch fell on the roof, then went hissing and scraping over it. Twice he thought he heard voices. His hammering heart lodged in his throat.

He moaned when the headlights of Albert Rose's truck swept across the bedspring-covered window.

If I had the axe — Damn fool! Took it back outside. Butcher knife! Better than nothing. Knocked it on the floor when I — where?

He crawled about, patting cautiously in the dark.

Spoons — Fork — Table knife — Plate — *Gotta* have it. Even if I gotta light the lamp.

He was setting the globe on the steadying flame when a voice roaring above the wind transfixed him with terror. "Macgregor, you little bastard, open that door. I'm gonna learn you — !"

A heavy shoulder crashed the door. Once. Twice. Terror sent André ranging the room like a caged coyote. At the third crash the door burst inwards. The chair braced under the knob collapsed, the back splintering from the seat. As Rose came charging in through the door, André sprang to get past him, hoping to escape into the night. He fell over the broken chair. Bellowing, Rose was on to him.

It was over in two minutes. Delivering one last brutal kick to his ribs with a steel-toed boot Rose growled, "Now, you goddamn little breed, get this through your head. You be outta here before morning, because, by Christ, if I ever catch you around here again, I'll kill you."

He turned, gave the bed spring propped against the window a contemptuous boot and brought it crashing down.

André heard Joey cry, but it seemed far away. Very far away. He sank into a pool of concentric black circles, rose from it briefly, then sank into it again. The next thing he remembered was vomiting. Helplessly. Vomiting and vomiting. His nose gushed blood, and every breath was an agony.

Cold! Snow — Get out! Said — Said — he kill me. Gotta get — Bl — Blood nose — Gotta, gotta get — Glass — Busted bones —

He was on hands and knees, head hanging. Salty saliva poured from his mouth to join the blood pouring from his nose. The black circles threatened him again. "No, no! He kill me. Gotta — go."

It was a year, ten, a lifetime before he could pick the parka up and get it on. "Can't — *Gotta!* He'll kill me. Kill me — "

He didn't remember leaving the shack. When he came to something like consciousness, he was staggering along with the wind tearing at him, his shoes laden with gumbo, and wet snow melting on his face. He held something in his hand; what, he couldn't see, but he was compelled to hang on to it. Suddenly he was on firm footing, and as though by some weird connection his head cleared.

Highway. I'm hurt bad. Nose busted. Ribs — Hide someplace — Johnny Crane, he'd — What's in my hand? Chickadee's scarf — Wrap around my head —

He was caught in the twin cones of a car's headlights. He floundered to the edge of the highway. The vehicle passed, splattering him with slush.

Brake lights flared, and the car slowly backed toward him.

"Hey, fella, you picked one hell of a night to hitch hike. Hop in back."

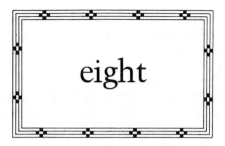

eight

Without thinking, André opened the door and eased himself into the car.

"Scarf wrapped right around your head, huh?" the driver remarked. "Good idea on a night like this. Where you heading?"

"St. Paul." It was the first name that came to mind.

"Must be in a hurry to get there to be out hitching on a night like this."

The woman in the front seat beside the driver hadn't looked at André when he got into the car. She didn't look at him now. She snapped forward and turned the volume up on the car radio. Violins backed by a symphony orchestra fairly pierced the ears.

"Holy smoke, Jean!" the driver protested.

"George, I *was* listening."

"'Okay. Okay." He sniffed resentfully and eased the car out onto the snow-thick highway.

The woman turned the volume down on the radio and lay back in the seat, eyes closed.

André sat with clenched jaws, breathing shallowly against the pain in his ribs. He eased himself into a slightly more tolerable position and made himself as inconspicuous as possible.

St. Paul? Jeez! But I had to get away. That sonofabitch'll kill me if—Sick! Goddamn bones full of busted glass. Wanna puke —Keep still, maybe—Good thing them two never got a look at my face. Blood from hell to breakfast. Take it easy. Maybe—

After a time the nausea subsided. Music and the monotonous hum of the car's engine lulled him. There were moments when he came close to dozing. He felt the car pull off the highway. The rough gravel in front of an all-night café jolted his damaged ribs excruciatingly, and the garish red and green neon sign played devilish tricks with his eyes.

"Shall we wake him up?" Jean asked.

"Well, this is St. Paul. That's where he said he was going. Could stake him to a cup of coffee."

The dome light snapped on before André could pull the scarf up to cover his face. The woman was staring at him. There was a small, shocked silence before she gasped, "George! My God — Look."

"Jesus Christ! What happened to you?"

"Guy smashed me in the face. Guess I got a couple of shiners, huh?" He eased himself toward the door and took hold of the handle. His eyes were so swollen he was having difficulty seeing what he was doing.

The couple exchanged glances. "Stay put," George ordered. "We're taking you to the hospital."

"Nah! It's nothin' — "

George didn't answer. He put the car in gear and headed down the dark streets of the sleeping town. He stopped the car in the parking area beside the hospital and said, "I'll go get help, Jean. You phone the police."

Cops, he said? The sonofabitch, I—

Before they had disappeared into the building André was out of the car. He could scarcely see, could breathe only through his mouth, and his ribs hurt fearfully, but he forced himself to a shuffling run. Around the hospital, through back alleys, across a road, under a barbed-wire fence, and into a deep patch of bush. There he stopped, gasping and quivering with snow melting on his face.

Cold — Can't stand here. Gotta hole up. Somewhere —

The lights of the town cast an eerie glow into the snow-filled sky which reflected onto the farm fields beyond. André spotted a freshly threshed straw pile in a stubble field. He made for it, steps wavering, his feet numbing with cold. He burrowed into the straw until he was completely covered, then rid himself of his sodden shoes and socks. He was shivering like a wet dog.

Then he remembered.

Joey! For christsake—Coulda wandered off in the snow. Don't remember leaving the shack. Maybe I should—Oh, hell, what's the use? What can I do now?

All that night he lay in the straw, dozing fitfully, and seeking more comfortable positions for his battered body. He came to full wakefulness in cold, clear starlight. From the position of the Big Bear he knew that dawn was approaching. He crawled out of his nest, brushed straw off himself and wondered, What the hell am I gonna do. Starving. And sixty dollars in my pocket. But somebody spot me looking like this, they'll phone the Mounties. Don't want trouble with them bastards.

If it wasn't for this fucking snow I could find a creek. Wash the blood off my clothes and clean my face.

He burrowed into the straw and found his shoes. It was a painful procedure, putting them on and tying the laces.

Ribs hurt like a bitch. Well, no use sitting here shivering. Looks like it might warm up today. Wonder if I can find the garden before that farmer starts stirring around?

Jeez! I wonder what happened to Joey? he fretted as he crossed the stubble field toward the farm house. He was relieved that a dog did not begin to yap as he circled around behind the buildings trying to locate a garden in the beginning dawn. He wrenched carrots out by their snow-cold stalks, knocked mud from them, and wolfed them as they were.

Three milk cows stood in a pole corral regarding him with mild interest.

Milk. If I had a can — Or a beer bottle.

He crept around the corner of the barn. A gas barrel stood beside the fenced off yard of the house.

Garbage. Be cans —

He cautiously climbed the fence so as not to make the wire creak, found a Campbell's soup can among the garbage, and made it back over without mishap.

On his second attempt, the gentlest of the cows allowed him to approach. He drank three cans full of steaming milk, then went back to the straw stack. The sun was rising as he burrowed into the straw.

The snow disappeared and by the afternoon it was as warm as a summer day. André crossed the stubble field and walked down a country road until he found a pasture with a small, muddy creek running through it. He followed the creek until he found a south-facing sun trap in the bank, and there set about cleaning himself.

Jeez! My ribs are sore, he thought as he knelt down and slopped water over his face. Well, anyhow I can see again, and my nose ain't too bad. Long as I don't touch it.

His stomach growled hollowly as he picked his washed shirt from a chokecherry bush where he had hung it to dry in the sun.

When I get into a café, I'm gonna eat four hamburgers and two *tons* of chips. Then what?

He buttoned his shirt and shoved the tail into his pants.

What? Whatever I want. Drift around. See the country. Sixty bucks in my jeans. Wish I had the other four hundred and something that old bastard of a Father Pépin's sitting on, but I ain't going back for it. Either he'll catch me and shove me in that technical school, or Rose'll catch me and —

He climbed over the fence and headed down the road that led to the highway. The sun was warm; the trees a riot of bronze and gold with scarlet underbrush at their feet.

I'm a free bird. Don't have to do *nothing,* he thought as he stood on the highway, thumb extended while cars whizzed by him, buffeting him with the wind of their passage. Finally a big red Buick pulled over onto the shoulder and waited while he trotted after it.

Two men occupied the front seat. The driver turned to stare at André. "Good Lord, what happened to you?"

André hesitated with the car door in his hand. "I'm — I'm okay."

"You sure?"

"Yeah."

"Where you going?"

"Well, I — "

"We're headed for Edmonton."

"Edmonton, huh? That's great." What the fucking hell made me say that? Never seen a city. Don't know —

"Are you getting in?"

"Huh? Oh, yeah. Sure."

Several times during the next couple of hours, André glanced at the speedometer. The needle hovered on eighty-five. Farms, villages, and scrubby sections of woodland slid past. The men scarcely spoke to each other, so he was startled when the driver remarked to his companion, "Well, Tony, there's Edmonton. Be home in good time for supper."

Edmonton? All I can see is three big, square buildings. And some fog, or smoke.

He was both relieved and disappointed. Then he noticed that traffic was beginning to pick up. They passed a number of small businesses strung out untidily on either side of the highway. Then he spotted an enormous, low grey building to his left. More cars than he had ever seen in one place stood in the huge parking lot surrounding it. NORTHGATE SHOPPING CENTRE.

Jeez!

When he turned from gaping at this wonder, he realized with a quickening heart that they were in the city.

Cars! Where'd they all come from? That's a city bus. Father Pépin says it cost two bits to ride—Houses—How'd a fella find his way around?

Suddenly, he was frightened.

Buildings — God! Clean to the sky.

He had counted twenty-three stories of the CN Tower when the driver asked him where he wanted to get out.

"Dunno," he gulped.

The car dipped into an underpass and came out in the roar of the city's heart.

The driver pulled the Buick in to the curb beside Eaton's store. "This is about as close to the centre of town as you can get," he said.

André crawled out and closed the car door.

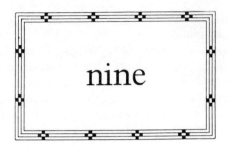

nine

It was five o'clock. André had never seen so many people or so many cars. The noise was terrifying. A long-haired hippie, barefoot, and in blue jeans, calling back to his girl friend, and walking without looking where he was going, blundered into him. He gave a sign with two fingers raised and said, "Hey, man! Peace!" André, attempting to avoid him, blundered into an old lady with two shopping bags.

"Mind yourself!" she snapped.

André backed against the plate glass window of the store, crowding between two well-dressed working girls. One turned to look at him and exchanged a glance with her companion, who made a wry face. They moved down the sidewalk away from him. One said something to the other and they examined him with hostile eyes before turning their shoulders on him.

He was wobble-kneed with weariness, and so hungry he was light headed.

What the fucking hell got into me to come here? Dunno where to go. Dunno who to ask. Don't even know how to cross the street so a car don't run me down. And if I cross the street, where am I going?

He sidled along to the corner of the store where he stood studying the traffic signals.

Cars go on the green light and stop on the red. Well, any damn fool knows that, but I never knew people gotta wait until the white man flashes, and they stop when the red hand goes up. How come cars turn on a red light? Don't get it, but I can't stand here all night. I got money in my pocket, and if I walk I'll find a café.

He stepped into a crowd crossing 102nd Avenue and gained the opposite sidewalk without mishap. He walked down the west side of 101st Street, gazing up at the confusing conglomeration of signs until he spotted the King Edward Bar and Grill.

Grill? That's a café.

He stepped onto the rubber mat with his hand extended to push the glass door open, but it swung inward without his touching it.

"What the hell?"

"Are you going in?" Two businessmen in smartly tailored suits all but stood on his heels looking at him impatiently. He stepped through the door to get out of their way and found himself in the red-carpeted, walnut-panelled lobby of the hotel. He had never seen such magnificence. There was a canary singing somewhere in the subdued light. Genteel voices murmured and traffic noise faded into the background. The businessmen looked at his expression, amusement in their eyes, and moved on.

An old man sat on a couch against the wall, his hands resting on the head of a cane set between his feet. A potted palm stood beside the couch, the first André had ever seen outside of the movies.

"Thought this was a café," he muttered, approaching the old man. "The sign said — "

"Yes, there's a café, but — " He picked up the stub of a cigar from an ash tray and lit it, examining André through the smoke. "First time in town, son? Well, look — " He pointed through the window, "If I were you, I'd walk three or four blocks down that way and find a café. Cheaper, and you'd feel more at home."

"Yeah?" He glanced about. "Yeah, well — thanks."

He turned to go out of the same door by which he had entered just as two gabbling matrons stepped on the rubber mat outside. The door swung in, nearly smacking him in the face.

"Can't you read?" one of the women asked, "There's the exit."

Feeling foolish, André slouched through the indicated door.

Jeez! What's happened? Hardly any cars. Don't need a traffic light to cross the street now.

A policeman stood against the hotel, examining him with

hard, blue eyes, as he stood at the curb gathering himself for a sprint.

"Whaddya think you're doing?"

"Just crossin' the — "

"Not there you don't. Down to the corner, unless you want a jay-walking ticket."

Goddamn place. What'd I come here for? Only person that's said a decent word to me was that old guy with the cigar.

When he rounded the corner of 97th Street, he saw two young Indian women talking to a white man.

"Fifteen," the man said stubbornly. He hawked and spat on the sidewalk.

The prettiest one giggled. "Twenty."

"Aw, shit!" He flapped his hand and shuffled off down the street.

André sidled up to the girls. "There a café around here?"

The least attractive one examined him with flat, uninterested eyes. "Across the street. See?" She smiled, exposing a row of rotten teeth. "You wanna zig-zig? Ten dollar?"

He shook his head. He was not walking quite straight. He entered a café and sat down on a stool at the counter. A Chinese came up to him and asked abruptly, "Whaddya want?"

"Two hamburgers, lots of chips, and coffee."

When the Chinese returned with the food he stood well back of the counter with the two plates in his hands. "You pay now."

"Haven't et yet," André protested, almost choking on his own saliva.

The Chinese was adamant. "Pay now."

André dug the roll of money out of his pocket and threw a five on the counter. The Chinese slid the plates across to him and picked up the money. He hesitated, then leaned down and said in a low voice, "You never been in the city before?"

André shook his head.

The Chinese laughed as though embarrassed and pointed to André's hand, which still held the roll of bills. "Better if you don't show all your money."

Jeez! Stupid. Soon as I eat I'm going in the can and stick most of this money in my shoe.

As he was finishing his third hamburger a shadow fell across him. He turned to look into the broad grin of a familiar face.

"Gary! Gary One Blanket! Well, I'll be — "

"Isaac Macgregor's kid. André, ain't it?"

Gary One Blanket was a bad character. Even Isaac admitted that, but André could have thrown his arms around the man and hugged him at that moment.

"What you doin' in du city?" Gary asked, then eyeing him critically, "Who punch you in du nose? He sure smash you good."

"Guess so," André admitted, feeling his nose tenderly and attempting an unsuccessful sniff.

"What you doin' in du city?" One Blanket persisted.

"Dunno. Just come in a little while ago. Guess I'll get a job."

"Job, shit! Who you think gives you a job."

"Same kinda guy that gives you one."

Gary giggled until he shook all over.

"Where does a guy start — ?"

One Blanket was not listening. A young Métis woman had entered the café. She was heavily made up, her eyelids coloured the same incongruous shade of green that Chickadee had smeared on herself the night she brought the garnet sand from across the lake. She wore a short purple dress, cut so low in front that the tops of her breasts bulged out. A heavy silver-coloured cross hanging from a chain around her neck half buried itself between them. There was something about her that reminded André of Simone.

Gary beckoned her imperiously with a jerk of his head, perched one buttock on a stool, leaned a forearm on the counter, and watched her approach with narrowed eyes.

"C'mon," he said sharply, turning the palm of his hand upwards and opening it without removing his elbow from the counter.

She reached into the top of her brassière, brought out some bills and laid them in his hand. As he counted the money, holding it under the shadow of the counter she muttered sullenly, "I wanna eat."

"I say when you eat." He glanced toward a white-faced fellow in a booth in a corner who was watching them from under his brows. "Dat Jack guy. He's waitin' for you."

The girl looked toward the booth, then crowded close to One Blanket in an attitude both pleading and defiant. "Not that bastard, Gary. He's mean."

"Cut du shit. Dere's a twenty in it if you treat him right. Get going."

"Gary —!"

"You ain't hearin' good tonight?"

The girl bit her bottom lip and backed off. She glanced from One Blanket to the man in the corner then with a conciliatory hunch of her shoulders, and an expression more grimace than smile, gestured with her head toward the café door and walked out.

Abruptly, the white-faced man rose, threw two dollars on the counter, and followed her.

One Blanket turned, grinned at André and jogged him with his elbow. "*Dose* du guys I work for. Got three girls. Dey're good or I beat du shit outta dem."

"She says that guy's mean."

"Christ! Don't take no crap from her. Rebecca'll be t'rough wid her John now. Want a liddle? Twenty-five. Rebecca knows some tricks — "

"Nah."

"Broke?"

"No, I got — "

"Well, have a liddle fun. What you come to town for? Rebecca'll — "

"Nah. Say, where'd a guy get a place to sleep?"

"Sleep? Whaddya wanna sleep for? Let's go down du street for a coupla beers. Gotta meet Josie — "

"Ain't eighteen. Can't go into the beer — "

"Jeez! You're sure green from du sticks!" Gary went into a fit of supressed asthmatic laughter. "In dis town, if you look eighteen, dey don't ask no questions. Long as you got du money."

"Nah. I gotta sleep. Where's a good place? Cheap."

"Good place? Cheap — ?" He snickered at some private thought, and jerked his thumb over his shoulder. "Down dere two, t'ree blocks. Du Macdonald across du street. Dat's good place."

André was glad to leave One Blanket. He had never liked him. He knew that in some way Gary was poking fun at him now, but he was too tired to worry about it. The prospect of a bed, any bed, was too alluring.

He walked down Jasper Avenue, which was transformed to a tunnel of reddish-gold by the setting sun. Before he had gone two blocks he spotted the red neon sign on the side of the Macdonald Hotel. The huge old sandstone building with its copper-turretted roof was terrifyingly forbidding.

Me go in *there*? That's why the sonofabitch was laughing.

He went back down to 97th Street and stood on the corner until he gathered enough courage to ask a young guy dressed in working clothes and carrying a lunch bucket where he might get a room.

"Lots of 'em down this street. There's signs in the windows, 'Rooms for Rent'. Just go knock on the door."

André walked four blocks before he spotted a water-stained sign in the window of a huge old house with a sagging wooden porch. An overgrown carragana hedge snagged at his sleeve as he made his way up the walk. A hard-faced woman with a mop of dyed red hair answered his knock.

"Room? You got a sign."

She pursed her lips and examined him. "Well, I got a room, but you look like — I don't stand for no fightin'."

When he made no reply she backed out of the doorway, clutching the faded blue chenille wrapper tight about her throat and gestured him to follow. She led him through a kitchen smelling overpoweringly of fried onions, down worn basement stairs, through a cluttered laundry room, and into a dingy basement bedroom with a sagging cot in one corner. The only other furniture was a green-painted kitchen chair standing against one wall, and an old-fashioned oak bureau with a murky, distorted mirror hanging above it.

"Twenty dollars for the week and a ten dollar damage deposit."

"Damage?"

"You get that back when you pull out. If nothing's busted."

Jeez! Half my money —

"Just want a room for the night."

"Don't rent rooms for the night. And pay is in advance."

Should see if I can't do better than this, but I'm so goddamn tired, and my ribs are hurting like a bugger.

He shrugged, peeled off thirty dollars, and handed it to her. "There's a bathroom around the corner there. And I don't stand for no broads, nor no liquor."

When he heard her footsteps clattering up the stairs, he sank down on the bed. But for the urgent need to relieve himself, he would have stretched out upon it. Instead, he tip-toed into the laundry room and looked about until he spotted a door which he assumed must lead to the bathroom.

Wash bowls, urinals, and toilets he had used in various cafés and service stations, but he had never been in a proper bathroom. He closed the door behind him. As he stood using the toilet he stared at the bathtub.

Jeez! I wonder—What if that old broad—? Nah! There's a lock on the door. Well, by God, I'm gonna.

He shucked his dirty clothes, left them in a heap on the floor, climbed into the tub and filled it to the slop point. He soaped his body, scrubbed his hair, then stretched out in the tub to frown at the multi-coloured bruises on his ribs and explore them tenderly with his fingers.

Wonder what my face is like?

When he looked in the mirror while he was towelling himself he stopped in amazement.

God! Bastard busted my nose for sure. No wonder everybody's looking at me funny.

He turned back to his clothes on the floor. The washing in the creek had done little for them. They reeked of stale sweat, and several blood stains were still much in evidence.

Could wash 'em. Hang 'em in the room. They'd be dry by morning.

He dumped the whole mess into the bathtub. When he had finished wringing the clothes, and made certain the coast was clear, he scuttled through the basement and into his bedroom, and spread the clothes over the chair and the bureau to drip on the floor. It didn't occur to him to drain the bathtub, hang up the towels, or wipe up the puddles on the bathroom floor.

Bed's nothing special, he thought, as he eased into it. But it's a bed.

The room was in the south-west corner of the house. He didn't waken until the sun was creeping across the floor the following afternoon. His clothes were dry, and because he had spread them carefully, not badly wrinkled.

Pretty good, he congratulated himself, as he dressed. I gotta remember to buy a comb, and one of them toothbrushes. Sister Bridget claims that if a guy brushes his teeth every day they don't —

There was a hard, imperious rap on the door. The red-headed woman stood there. "What the hell do you think you're—?" She broke off, staring at the bureau, its coat of varnish now white from the load of wet clothes. "My bureau! What kind of a—? Leave the bathroom looking like a herd of pigs camped there— Wrecked my bureau! Well, that's it. You get the hell outta here right now."

"Never knew wet clothes'd—" He gestured helplessly toward the bureau. "I'll clean the floor, and—Jeez! Never thought about the bathroom."

"From the looks of things, you never used one before." She stepped out of the doorway and gestured toward the stairs. "C'mon. Out."

"I paid for the week."

"Prove it. In a week you'd have holes knocked in the walls and the shingles ripped off the roof."

"But I paid—"

"You can't prove nothin'. Get out before I call a cop."

Feeling betrayed and utterly miserable, he slunk past her, up the stairs, and out onto the street.

Thirty dollars! Got less then thirty left, and no place to sleep tonight. Gotta find a job, but where does a fella—?

He was overwhelmed with homesickness.

If there was a patch of bush. Someplace where a fella could—

As he was about to enter the café where he had eaten the night before, he met a policeman coming out leading a sullen Indian woman by the wrist.

"Where'd—Where'd a fella get a job?" André managed.

The policeman glowered at him suspiciously. "On the level?"

"Level? Well, sure."

"Manpower." He reeled off a string of numbers which André supposed must be an address, but they were meaningless to him.

At that moment, the Indian woman wrenched out of the policeman's grasp and darted across the street. A car screeched to a stop to avoid hitting her, and the car following rammed into the first one with a mighty metallic crash. The policeman cursed, ignored the accident, and galloped after the fleeing woman.

André was left no wiser than he had been before. It was the little Chinese in the café who finally directed him.

The Manpower placement officer was a kindly-looking, harried man with a deeply lined face and a receding hairline. He shook his head and pulled at his chin. "Look, I'll give it to you straight. You haven't got a chance of finding a job in Edmonton right now. I can't even place people with skills and experience."

"I'm a good pump jockey."

"Pump jockey — Well, if anybody *needed* a pump jockey — " He frowned and rapidly released and depressed the point of his pen. "You're Métis, aren't you? Well, it's not fair, I never said it was, but we have one hell of a time placing you people. If I were you, kid, I'd head for the bush." He shrugged. "Hang around Edmonton, and the first thing you know you'll be in trouble. That's the way it goes — but if you tell anybody I said that, I'll swear up and down I didn't." He studied the file of information he had taken from André. "Grade twelve?" he probed. "Matriculation?" There was a pause. He looked off into the middle distance and thrust his lips out, considering.

Gonna start in on me — University, or some damn thing —

"What—? Anythin' wrong with askin' for work at a construction job?"

A wry smile twisted up one corner of the officer's mouth. "Nothing wrong with asking."

"Where'd there be one?"

"City's full of them. You just have to walk."

No use hunting for construction jobs tonight, André thought when he got out of the office. It's just about quitting time.

He sat in the lobby of a cheap, 97th Street hotel until the night clerk chased him out when the beer parlour closed. Then he wandered about the centre of the city until he found the bus depot. The first thing he saw when he entered was a young Indian couple cornered by a security guard.

"Can't loiter here," the guard was saying. "You're not going anywhere, you're not meeting anybody, so move along."

The woman, her face anxious, picked up an old brown paper shopping bag. Her belly was big with pregnancy. Her husband rolled a cigarette, lit it, and without looking at her, slouched toward the door. She coughed hollowly and shuffled after him.

The guard looked sharply at André.

To buy time, he began studying the huge board with the departure and arrival time of the buses. An idea hopped into his mind.

If I had a ticket on a bus leaving tonight he couldn't kick me out.

He found a bus leaving for Spruce Grove, a village just outside Edmonton, at six thirty in the morning. Armed with the ticket, he found a vacant chair, made himself as inconspicuous as possible, and dozed fitfully until sunrise. After a breakfast of toast and coffee in the bus depot café, he began tramping the streets looking for construction sites.

By five o'clock that afternoon he had been refused employment by fourteen different construction foremen, and his boots, cheap in the first place, were worn through at the soles. Then the sole of one boot parted from the upper, which forced him to walk swinging one leg, while the wrecked shoe slap-flapped the sidewalk at every step. Before closing time, he made it back to a small, shabby store he had passed on Whyte Avenue which was not too unlike the country stores he was used to.

The clerk was kindly enough, but he insisted that André buy socks before being allowed to try on boots. When he walked out of the store he had fourteen dollars and twenty three cents in his pocket. He arrived back in the 97th Street area at seven o'clock that night. The first person he met, slouching along beside the W.W. Arcade, was Gary One Blanket.

"Hey, André! How you like du Macdonald?"

"Piss on you!"

Gary giggled. "Liddle joke. Don't be sore. Where you been hidin'? Never seen you today."

"Where's a guy find a job around here?"

"Job? Don't be dumb. Ain't no jobs."

"Gotta find somethin'. I'm down to fourteen dollars."

"Fourteen dollars? Jeez, man, you're rich!"

"Got kicked out of a roomin' house, slept in the bus depot. And I been sloggin' around all day lookin' for work. Fuckin' cement —"

"I give you a room. Good room. Cheap."

"How much?"

"Two bucks."

"Where's your women?"

"Johns take 'em for du night." He giggled slyly. "Dat's what you need—Two, t'ree whores. Don't see me bustin' my ass on no fuckin' construction job, huh?"

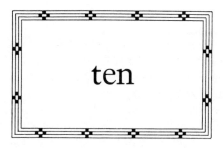

ten

Don't wanna sleep in Gary One Blanket's goddamn bed. But I can't walk all day, then buy tickets to nowhere so I can sit up in the bus depot all night.

"Two bucks, you say?"

"'Nodder buck and we buy a case of beer." He clapped André chummily on the shoulder. "Have a little party, you and me. Maybe play a liddle stook, huh?"

André was too tired to argue. He handed over three dollars and tagged behind Gary while he bought beer, then followed him back down the street and climbed a long, wooden stairway to enter three filthy rooms over a second hand shop.

"Where do I sleep?"

"Sleep? Shit! Sleep when you're dead. We gonna have liddle party." He ripped the top off the beer case, extracted two bottles and knocked the caps off on the edge of the kitchen table. He handed one to André, then drank off half of what his contained before removing his lips from the bottle. He belched mightily. "Jeez! Dat's good stuff, huh?"

André, with the untouched bottle in his hand, stared at a cheap calendar with the picture of a naked girl in a suggestive pose.

Gary snickered. "Nice piece of ass, ain't it? Only, she's paper. You try Rebecca. Ten dollar for you. Anythin' for a friend."

Fourth of September. Them classes starting in Earth Resources tomorrow. And here I am, no job, damn near broke, drinking beer with Gary One Blanket.

Dodie Rose's vicious words came back to him. "You're like all the rest of them. Gonna do wonders and shit cucumbers, but you'll end up on welfare, wiping your ass on pages out of the Eaton's catalogue."

Who gives a fart what she says? But I'll dump One Blanket, soon as I get a job. If I had a little money — Well, Jeez! Father Pépin's sitting on damn near five hundred dollars. If I wasn't so goddamn scared of Albert Rose —

One Blanket went into one of the other rooms and returned with a pack of cards. He shoved some dirty mugs to one end of the table and set the pack in front of André. "Wanna deal?"

All his life André had watched stook games. He had played it himself for pebbles or matches when he was a small boy, and for pennies later, when he had pennies to spare. He considered himself good at it. Gary suggested they play for nickel pots. André was both confident and eager. He won steadily for the first half hour. Then One Blanket, claiming that he wanted to change his luck, suggested they play for dimes. Suddenly, André began to lose. As time went on he was convinced that One Blanket was cheating. But although he watched until his vision distorted, he could not catch him.

Damned if I'm quitting. When I catch him —

He had drunk four bottles of beer and was down to his last fifty cents. "Well, you about cleaned me. I'm quitting," he muttered, struggling to conceal his resentment. "Where's my sack? Gotta get some sleep. I'm headin' for the bush in the morning."

"Bush? What you do dere?"

"Get five hundred dollars Father Pépin's keepin' for me. And then — " He shrugged. "I dunno."

"Fadder Pépin keepin' five hundred dollar for you? Bull shit!"

"Ain't bull shit."

One Blanket looked at him from under his brows. His eyes narrowed slyly. "You got five hundred bucks?"

"Yeah."

Feet clattered on the stair below them. "Leggo of me, you bastard!" a woman yelled. There were sounds of scuffling, and loud thumps. It sounded as though someone had fallen down the stairs.

One Blanket was through the door and down the stairs before André was on his feet. In a moment he was back, shoving Clara, the girl André had seen in the café, in front of him. She was holding the back of her hand to her mouth, which was bleeding profusely.

"Ain't satisfied with screwin', the sonofabitch! He — He —
Then he follows me home. Smashes me in du face — "

"Du money!" One Blanket demanded.

"Don't give me no money. He — "

Gary grabbed her by the arm, yanked her off balance, and
slapped the side of her face so hard her head spun around.
Droplets of blood from her cut mouth spattered over the table.
One landed on André's lip. She threw up her free arm to ward off
another blow. "Don't Gary! Don't — " she cried.

He shoved her against a chair. She fell over it and landed in a
cringing heap against the radiator. When he advanced on her,
André thought he was going to kick her, but he stood over her
and snarled, "You work for money, you bitch, or I t'row you out
on your ass. Now, get dat goddamn mouth fixed and get to bed. I
ain't t'rough wid you yet."

He came back to the table where André was sitting and said in
a friendly, conspiratorial tone, "Five hundred dollar, huh?
Might be I go wid you tomorrow. You and me get two, t'ree more
girls. Get nice house, not dis dump. Jeez! We be rich like du
white bastards. Do nothing but drink beer and play stook. You
got two sisters, ain't you? Dat one, Simone—Seen her in town.
And du liddle one. Now, dere's a good start, and wid my t'ree
bitches — " He winked. "Beats du fuckin' construction job."

Clara picked herself up and shuffled into the bathroom off the
kitchen. There was a sound of rushing water.

One Blanket moved toward a room that was in darkness
beyond. He jerked his head toward the bathroom where Clara
was still splashing water. "Wanna ball dat bitch when I'm
t'rough?"

André shook his head. "Where do I sleep?"

"Couch over dere."

It was an ancient, greasy relic, with the stuffing spilling out of
the arms, and coil springs pushing through the cushions. André
stretched out on it, fully dressed except for his boots, and tried to
make himself comfortable.

Jeez! Be glad to get outta here. Whatever I do with that five
hundred, I ain't throwing it in with Gary One Blanket and his
whores. Figures I'm gonna fetch Chickadee in. Fuck him!

Any luck, and I'll be home by suppertime tomorrow. Sneak
around and see Father Pépin first thing. He'll know if Albert
Rose is around. Jeez! Father's gonna give me shit about that

geology course. But I ain't going. To hell with it.

A spring from one of the cushions poked into his tender ribs. He shifted his weight. He was drifting toward sleep when he saw Clara creep out of the bathroom and slink toward the room where One Blanket had disappeared.

She's sure like Simone. Simone with the guts kicked out of her.

There was no door separating the rooms. Before Gary One Blanket was through with Clara, André was plugging his ears to block out the sounds.

Sonofabitch! Boar pig! 'Nough to make a guy puke. He ain't *human*.

He lay for a long time staring up into the darkness. Clara was still whimpering when he went to sleep.

The screech of a fire engine passing down the street wakened him at dawn. He tried to go back to sleep, but there was a peculiar odour in the room, faintly sweet, rather sharp, and a trifle nauseous. He knew the smell, yet he could not identify it. The spring that had tortured his ribs all night forced him to turn over. He opened his eyes. Three feet from the couch Clara lay sprawled on the floor. She seemed to be staring at him. He sat up. His feet landed in a pool of congealing blood. He saw a knife, and Clara's wrist, slashed to bone. There was a dime store ring on one of her fingers. A facet of its blue stone was caught by the sun.

He gagged. "Gary! Gary, for christsake — "

One Blanket appeared, wearing only a suit of dirty, cheap cotton underwear. His face was heavy and sleep-sullen. He blinked at Clara's body.

"Du stupid bitch! What we gonna do?"

"*We*? I never — "

"You better call du cops."

"You go to hell!"

While One Blanket stared at the body André yanked socks and shoes over his bloody feet, fled down the stairs, and out into the street. The only person he saw was an elderly Chinaman padding along with a newspaper-wrapped bundle under his arm.

André turned straight north. For two blocks he forced his pace down to a walk, then he ran until searing torture in his lungs forced him to walk again. Close to the city limits he saw a long-distance trucker gassing up at a service station.

eleven

The village of Fish Lake straggled for a mile along the lake shore. At one end of it, high on a hill commanding a magnificent view of the lake and its promontories stood the Roman Catholic church, and the rectory; at the other end, a number of Métis shacks, Isaac's among them, and the hastily constructed near-shacks of the poor whites and itinerant workers like Albert Rose trailed off into the bush.

André asked the trucker to let him off beside a large area of natural bush a mile outside town. He knew that bush as well as he knew Rachel's face. If he met anyone passing through, it would not be Albert Rose, nor anyone likely to tell Albert Rose about having seen him there. It was a wild area, spotted with muskeg. One neck of it stretched to within a few hundred feet of the church property.

He hopped down into the ditch, skirted a soggy area with bullrushes, climbed the other ditch bank and was in the deep woods. It was almost sunset. The air held the suggestion of frost, the rot of high-bush cranberries, and the sharp, astringent cleanliness of new-fallen poplar leaves. He struggled through wild rose and willow underbrush and over deadfall until he came upon a familiar path.

Home. He marked the fall of a leaf, the tap of a woodpecker, the passage of a flock of song sparrows, feeding as they went. In a muskeg area a hundred yards away, he heard a faint splash and a rustling sound; he knew that a muskrat had climbed to the top of its den with a load of grass. His face lifted to the glowing autumn woods and the cloudless sky.

Jeez! The bush — Never gonna leave it. Ever.

He looked in the direction of the rectory.

Should go talk to him now, but—Feel like hell. So tired I could pull a pile of leaves over me and curl up under that tree. Can't face the old bugger tonight. I'm going home.

Friday night. Maybe Rose is laying in the grass outside the old man's shack waiting for me with a shotgun. Well — chance I gotta take.

He stayed in the bush until he saw a hunting owl silhouetted against the last vestiges of twilight, and his breath showed in white ghost-puffs on the chill of the coming night. An hour later, having made a wide circle through bush, across farm fields and through still more bush, he paused in the deep shadow of a clump of spruce trees across the road from Isaac's shack.

A waning, distorted moon rose from the lake radiating fingers of light across the water. It picked up the shack in its cold, sad light, and it picked up Rose's house.

Lamp's lit at our place, but the dump across the fence is dark. Wonder — ?

He listened very hard and caught the metal clink of a spoon on the edge of a pot.

Ma getting supper. His mouth flooded with saliva. Car on the road out in front. Impala, looks like. Who — ? Father Pépin! What the hell? Looking for me, or — ? Or what?

A shiver of apprehension went over him.

Nobody around Rose's house now. Sure of that. But I better get over close to the wood pile before the moon rises any higher.

Keeping the shack between himself and the Rose house, he ghosted across to become one with the shadow of the wood pile. He crouched there, mouth open, senses straining. A small breeze had sprung up. He could hear the faint complaint of a creaking door. He crawled along to the end of the wood pile, then stretched out to peer around it at the Rose house across the fence.

Door's open. Swinging in the wind. No truck!

He got to his feet, peering, head weaving.

Windows're busted. Sonofabitch took Dodie and the kid, and — He giggled in weak relief. Jake Averil's kids busted the windows already.

Tears stung behind his eyes. He was flooded with weariness. He stumbled as he rounded the shack and mounted the broken step.

The door knob was snatched from his hand when he reached

for it. Father Pépin and he stared speechlessly at each other. Then Rachel was between them, shoving the priest heedlessly aside as she drew André into the shack. Tears swam in her bloodshot eyes, and her fingers tenderly explored his battered face. "Scared he'd killed yah. Yah hurt? Bad hurt?"

"Shoulda seen me three days ago."

He stumbled across to the bed where he had slept beside Joey, and his shaking knees collapsed. He saw Chickadee and Isaac, but they seemed a long way off.

Father Pépin was staring at him. "Rachel," he said gravely, "perhaps I should bring Dr. Pêche —"

"No, Fadder!" She shook her head from side to side and caged her face with her fingers. "No more tonight. Can't stand no more."

Still the priest hesitated, a frown of indecision on his brows. "André, are you in trouble with the law?"

André slumped sideways on the bed and heaved a sigh so deep his aching ribs protested.

"I dunno, Father. Right now, I don't give a shit."

There was a fleeting moment before he fell into a black well of dreamless sleep when he realized that Joey was not there. No one had to tell him. Joey was dead.

Morning sunlight was streaming through the open door when Chickadee shook him awake. He opened his eyes to see Rachel standing beside the bed, a bowl of steaming stew in one hand, and a spoon in the other. "Better eat, André. Du priest be here pretty quick."

He swung his feet to the floor and sat up, elbows on knees, cheeks propped on the heels of his hands. "That night—Joey— Don't remember —"

"No use now," Rachel said wearily. "He's gone. You gonna eat or not?"

He didn't taste the stew, merely swallowed it.

From somewhere out on the lake, a loon cried. Another answered.

"Hollerin' for going," Chickadee said. "You be goin' again, too."

"Not me."

"Yeah, you. They're sayin' you're a smart fella."

"Yeah! Real smart fella!" He could see Rose's house framed in the window.

Except for those times when he was travelling, Father Pépin lived in his cassock; when he entered the shack he was wearing his black suit.

"Now then, André, this trouble with the police—Before the Mountie finds you 'ere, I wish to know. Everything."

André fumbled through his tale. He tried to meet the flame of the priest's eyes, but he could not do so. He was tortured by a need to relieve himself, but he could not make his needs known. He despised himself for his halting delivery, and the apologetic upward inflection of his sentences.

"This *is* the truth?"

"Yeah, Father. It's the truth."

The priest pursed his lips repeatedly. "Well, as for the beating you got from this Rose fellow— And Joey— 'ard lessons. Very 'ard. But bruises and broken ribs mend. I will 'ave Dr. Pêche check you over before —"

Before what, you old bastard? If you figure you're gonna take me —

"As for this terrible business in Edmonton — The girl was dead when you wakened. You should 'ave stayed. But you didn't."

Rivulets of chilly sweat trickled down André's ribs.

"Already you 'ave missed one day of classes at the technical school. We cannot expect more concessions." He turned to Rachel. "You 'ave 'is clothes and things prepared?"

"Father, I ain't —" André began.

"'Now, mark this. If the police call you in this affair with One Blanket and the girl, you 'ave to go. Otherwise it is best you stay clear of it." He grinned harshly. "There were times this week I thought that all I 'ave done for you—all my 'opes for you—" He spread his hands. "Chaff in the wind. But it is not so."

Sweet sufferin' Jesus! What can I say? He's got me. Dunno how I'm gonna stand it, but the old bastard's got me.

Chickadee trotted beside the open window of the car as it moved off. "You write me a letter sometime?"

In the bush where he had hidden the night before, vowing never again to leave it, he glimpsed a cow moose with its two calves, belly deep in a slough, their heads submerged among the lily roots. He strained back to watch them. They still had not lifted their heads when a curve of the road cut them from his sight.

twelve

André sat hunched in the seat beside Father Pépin, not lifting his gaze above his knees. The priest did not speak to him. He gripped the wheel with white-knuckled hands and stared unblinkingly at the road ahead. The speedometer wavered on thirty-five. For a full half-mile behind, cars, buses, and truckloads of cattle lined up, dangerous with their impatience to pass.

"You 'ave a driver's license?"

"Yeah. Drove Mason's truck."

Father Pépin pulled over onto the shoulder, traded places with him and promptly went to sleep.

Aside from the truck, the only vehicle André had ever driven was a hopeless old Ford Isaac had bought one time when he had been working at the saw mill. By contrast the Impala was a perfect dream of a car. In minutes he had picked up the feel of it and was cruising at sixty with the old priest snoring beside him. His black mood began to lift.

Jeez! What a boat. Like to goose her and see what she'd do. I'd give half my ass for —

"You like the car, hah?" Father Pépin was looking at him, one eye open. "Well, one day perhaps—When you 'ave a good job—" He sighed and settled down again. "Waken me before we get to Edmonton. I do not think you could manage the city traffic."

At three o'clock that afternoon, under a mackerel sky filtering sunlight, Father Pépin pulled into the visitors' parking area in front of the Northern Alberta Institute of Technology.

André followed him through the glass doors and down the green flagstone corridor to the general office. Dozens of young guys with piles of books under their arms brushed past. Girls in white lab coats hurried along chattering among themselves. Four older men, plainly instructors, marched abreast, intent on the words of one of the group who was gesticulating with both hands as he moved. Through the glass walls, and across the brilliant green grass of a court yard, André could see more glass and more corridors.

How the hell am I gonna find my way around here?

There was a confusing half-hour in the office with rapid instruction about courses, books, and the locations of class rooms and laboratories. The young woman who was leaning across the counter with a map of the institution in her hand, looked into André's face and smiled. "Mixed up?"

"Jeez! Yeah."

"It'll sort out in a few days. Ask for help if you're stuck. And get at your studies at once. You're late coming in. Three days here is like a month in high school. Have you a place to live?"

"He 'as," Father Pépin put in. "I shall take 'im there immediately."

It seemed they had driven through a thousand miles of streets before Father Pépin stopped the car in front of an untidy, two-story clapboard house. When they were half-way up the cement walk the door of the house burst open. Out came a tubby boy of about twelve followed by a yapping little floor mop of a dog. The lad examined André and Father Pépin, then hopped back into the house and bellowed, "Mom! The priest and that guy are here."

A dark woman came to the door, wiping her hands on a red and white gingham apron.

"Come in," she invited.

Three teen-agers appeared. A tall boy of about André's age grinned at him while a younger sister examined him through a curtain of blonde hair. A still younger girl ducked out of the house squealing teasingly "Oooh! Is he ever neat."

"Donna!" the mother reproved, laughing. She shook her head. "That kid! Now, about the room—" She trotted a few steps up a stairway and beckoned to André and Father Pépin. As they followed her up, and into a small bedroom, she said, "We charge sixty a month." She smiled at André. "And you'll be treated like one of the family."

André cleared his throat miserably. Suppose I pull some dumb stunt like in that boarding house?

"Tell you the truth, Mrs. Bayrock, I never lived in — in — "

"A modern city home," she supplied for him. "Well, there was a time I hadn't either. I'm Métis too, you know. Or did Father Pépin tell you?"

"Oh, Mom, do we have to go through this *my folks met the Mayflower* bit again?" the blonde girl protested.

"It's nothing to be ashamed of, Barbara." She turned to André. "The room suit you?"

He looked about wondering how he would ever cope with such magnificence.

"Perhaps you should explain the house rules, Mrs. Bayrock," Father Pépin said.

She smiled. "We don't make rules."

Father Pépin raised his eyebrows and hesitated as though he wanted to say something. Then, apparently thinking better of it, he shrugged, walked out of the room, and from half-way down the stairs, called, "André. I want a word with you."

Outside, he got into the car and motioned André in beside him. He took a manila envelope from his briefcase. "Your summer wages. Ask Mrs. Bayrock to 'elp you bank it. Write to tell me the number of the account. On the last day of each month I shall transfer ninety dollars to it. *If* you behave, and *if* your marks are satisfactory." He looked at André piercingly. "Make no mistake. I don't send you 'ere to waste my money and make a fool of yourself."

André turned away to hide his flaming face as the priest continued. "I 'ave taken care of the tuition. You buy your own clothes, books, and a bus pass. You 'ear me?" He moved restlessly. "And now, for me, it is the long journey home."

André was left standing on the short grass of the boulevard with his few possessions about his feet.

Dick, the eldest Bayrock boy, sauntered out of the house and scooped up the half-dozen tattered Time-Life books, then leaned down to peer into a mandarin orange crate full of rocks. He blinked. A puzzled frown knotted his brow, then with a shrug he hoisted one of the boxes and started for the house.

André, holding the manila envelope between his teeth, hoisted the other box onto one hip, the box of clothes onto the other, and followed.

"What's in the envelope?" Dick asked curiously as he set the box on André's bed.

"Summer wages. Pretty near five hundred — "

"Whew!"

Mrs. Bayrock had come in with a pile of clean towels. "I'll take care of it for you until you can get to the bank."

The youngest girl, Donna, spotted the rocks and tittered nervously.

"All right, you girls — Out," Mrs. Bayrock said crisply. "You know you are not to be in this room. I need help with supper, Barbara. And Donna, your room hasn't been tidied." She turned to the younger son. "Have you finished packing those carrots into the cold room, Ronnie?"

"Ah, Mom! I wanna — "

"Right now."

Ronnie made a wry face and dragged himself toward the stairs.

"Dick'll get you settled," Mrs. Bayrock said, turning back to André. "There'll be lots of things you don't understand — Things you don't know how to work. Don't suffer over them. *Ask.* We'll help." A baby began to cry somewhere down below. "Oh-oh! Thinks he's starving." She hurried out of the room, then called back from half-way down the stairs, "Supper in half an hour."

There was an awkward pause in the room.

"We'll be travelling to NAIT together," Dick offered self-consciously. "I'm in the Building Construction course."

"Yeah?"

Another pause.

"That bus ride clean across the city's gonna be a drag," Dick offered.

Again they had nothing to say to each other. To cover his embarrassment, André took out his package of tobacco and was about to roll a smoke.

"Hey, man," Dick said. "You better kick the habit. In the house, anyhow. Dad won't stand for it." He rose. "If you really want one we can go outside."

As they wandered about the garden Dick peppered him with rapid-fire and confusing advice. How to use a bus transfer. The cheapest place in town to buy clothes. How to keep in the good graces of Stockings, the little black dog. When André had finished his cigarette, Dick said, "And the automatic washer — Show you that right now."

As they were about to enter the house, Dick startled him again. "Hey, man! Shoes off at the door. Mom gets uptight about mud on the floor."

Jeez! For a place that's got no rules, there's sure a hell of a lot you're not supposed to do, André thought, struggling with a knot in his shoe lace.

He learned something besides how to use the washer while he was in the basement. Dick mentioned that his father was a maintenance man at an oil refinery.

"Good job," Dick told him, "except it's shift work. We gotta step light around here when he's sleeping in the daytime. That's the only time he gets sore at Mom for taking Welfare babies, if they howl when he's trying to sleep."

"Welfare babies?"

"Yeah. You know — Before somebody adopts them?"

He didn't know, but before he could pursue it, Mrs. Bayrock was calling them for supper. A heavy-set blond man, still in work clothes, was ensconced in an armchair when they came upstairs. He fixed André with a sharp appraising look, laid aside the *Edmonton Journal*, grinned and asked good-naturedly as he held out his hand, "Well, getting settled? I'm Sam Bayrock."

Damn funny, André puzzled, him not drinking beer when he's just come home from work. Never seen a guy like that.

Mrs. Bayrock stood beside the table in the dining alcove. "Sit in," she invited. "You here, André. This'll be your place."

"Hey, Mom, we gonna make out the work sheet tonight?" Ronnie asked as he slid into the chair beside André.

She laughed. "Let's not scare André before he's eaten a meal with us."

André was starving. It was all he could do to keep from dumping food on his plate, but no one else touched a dish. Mrs. Bayrock carried an earthenware teapot to her place, and when she was seated, nodded to Donna.

The girl bowed her head and said a hasty grace.

Jeez! If I'd started shovelling grub first thing I'da sure felt cheap. And what grub! Roast beef. Gravy. Hate peas and spuds, but they're eating 'em, so I better.

"What's for dessert, Mom?" Dick asked.

"Apple pie and ice cream."

On top of *this*? Do they eat like this all the time?

"Ronnie, you're holding your fork like a shovel. Like this. See?" Mrs. Bayrock said, "And take your spoon out of your cup." Oh, shit! Me too. Only reason I never had my spoon in my cup was that I wasn't drinking tea.

After they had finished their pie, Ronnie again brought up the question of the work schedule.

"Just as well get it over with, Sam," Mrs. Bayrock said.

"Yeah. Well, you know we're charging you sixty a month," Bayrock said, looking at André. "Going rate in town is between seventy-five and ninety. For pretty awful dumps, some of 'em. You're getting it cheap because we expect a little work out of you. Oh, don't panic. Nothing that's going to stop you studying. Just things that'll teach you how to look after a house. Bit of maintenance — Keeping your room, washing your clothes — Shovelling a little snow. Stuff like that."

"It's hard when you first come out of the bush," Mrs. Bayrock said. "I know. The family that looked after me when I came in to go to high school — " she broke off, laughing. "I don't know where the woman got the patience. I didn't know what a clock *was*. Months before I could live in the house properly, let alone help her. But she made me learn. If she hadn't—" She shrugged. "Maybe 97th Street."

André tried to picture her as one of Gary One Blanket's whores. He couldn't do it.

"Incidentally, you stay out of that part of town," Bayrock said sternly. "We had a girl here a couple of years ago. Doing fine till she started going down there in the bars."

Resentment stirred in André. "Think you're gonna turn me into a white man?"

"Not a white man. A Métis that can handle himself in the white man's world. There's quite a difference," the woman said levelly. "And don't kid yourself. The only way we're going to live at all is to learn to handle the white man's world. Gabriel Dumont and the good old buffalo days are gone."

André blinked at her.

"You know who I'm talking about?"

"No."

She rose from the table, went to a cupboard, took out a book, flipped it open and laid it in his hands.

A huge man in fringed buckskin stared back from the page, an inappropriately tiny rifle cradled in the crook of his left arm.

The eyes, fierce and direct as a hawk's, met André's with the force of a living glance.

"Louis Riel's general, guess you'd call him," Mrs. Bayrock said, "One tough baby. If he'd had the guns, and the Indians had backed him he might have run every white man clean back past Lake Winnipeg—If Riel had kept quiet and let him fight—If—If—" she laughed sourly. "Good thing poor old Gabriel never got it all together, for us. Because when the whites came back, and they would have, there'd have been no Métis left to *be* a problem."

"Mom, that work sheet—" Ronnie prodded.

"Oh, for heaven's sake! You afraid you're going to wash an extra dish?"

"I'll give you a hand if you want, Ronnie," André offered.

"Sucker!" Dick crowed in good-natured derision.

Sam Bayrock grinned. "Enough outta you, mister. And you better hit those books as soon as the table's cleared."

"Be all right if I read that book about that Dumont guy?" André asked as he picked up two dirty plates from the table. He turned to the sink and set the plates into it, scraps and all.

"Hey!" Ronnie remonstrated. "You gotta scrape 'em. And it's glasses first, then silver, then—"

"Just show him, Ronnie. Don't be so bossy," Mrs. Bayrock said. She turned to André. "Well, you can see there's lots to learn in the white man's world. Even down to the level of washing dishes properly."

"Nellie, that church meeting starts in half an hour," Bayrock said, "and I want to be on time."

"Just have to comb my hair and take off my apron. Donna, your turn to watch the babies tonight," she called into the living room. "They're clean and fed, so there'll be no problem. We'll be home by ten. Oh, and André, if that book interests you, read it by all means."

As soon as his parents had gone, Dick wiped the table and sat down with text books spread in front of him. There was a businesslike leave-me-alone-I'm-working air about him.

Donna appeared, opened the refrigerator and stared into it. She looked coyly at André, who was drying dishes, and said, "Why did you bring that box of rocks with you?"

"They're a collection if I ever get 'em mounted. Some of 'em pretty interestin'."

"Rocks?" Her voice arched incredulously.

"Sure. C'mon, I'll show you." He started for the stairs with Donna at his heels.

"Donna!" Dick said sharply, "You know what Dad said."

"Well, for Pete's sake," Donna protested, "we're only gonna look at rocks."

"If you wanna look at rocks you bring 'em down here. And anyhow, you got homework." He went back to his books with the calm air of an authority whose orders are not to be questioned.

Donna glowered at him for a moment, then flounced into the living room and sat down with a literature text.

André, feeling a bit deflated and resentful, picked up the book Mrs. Bayrock had lent him and went up to his room. He settled at the desk and began looking through his new text books, but he could not concentrate. Too much had happened during the day.

He stared at the room and its furnishings, tried the bed, opened the desk and bureau drawers one by one and wondered who would ever own enough things to fill them all. The house was silent, yet somehow breathing in a way he had never known before. It made him uneasy. He yawned nervously and kicked off his shoes.

Jeez, I'm tired. Feet stink. And them sheets — Never seen anything that white. Better take a bath. Do I have to ask somebody? Well, anyhow I know I gotta hang the towels up after, and not leave any puddles on the floor.

He came out of the bathroom half an hour later, clean and pleased with himself. He hesitated at the top of the stairs.

Wonder what the kids are doing? Sure like to go down. Nah, better not. Read that book about Gabriel something-or-other, maybe.

The book was little more than a glorified pamphlet. He read it in half an hour, then turned back to the portrait of the man and stared at it for a long time.

Gabriel Dumont, huh? Jesus! What a *guy*.

He heard the elder Bayrocks enter the house. There was a few minutes of conversation and activity. Then Mrs. Bayrock rapped on his door. "André, there's a can of Old Dutch cleanser and a sponge under the sink in that cupboard. After you have taken a bath, you clean the tub, okay?"

"All right," he gulped.

Can't I do *anything* right?

He shed his clothes, leaving them in a pile in the middle of the floor and slipped into bed. For a long time he listened to the forced air furnace cutting in and out, the purr of the refrigerator, and the chime clock striking. It was a noisy alien world. His heart ached with homesickness.

Never slept by myself in a room except that one time in that fucking boarding house. Door's shut, but I feel naked. Like somebody was looking right through me. Jeez! What I'd give to be back in the bush. Way back in the bush, with night coming, and the snow falling. Well, I ain't, so I guess I'm in for it.

thirteen

Sam Bayrock's knuckles, hard and sharp on the door the next morning, jerked him from sleep.

"C'mon, fella. Gotta be on that bus in an hour."

It was the beginning of a month-long nightmare.

Before he had finished his breakfast Dick was prodding, "Get a move on, André. And don't forget your lunch bag."

The complexity of the technical school baffled him. He lost himself in the corridors. It was a long time before he learned to take care of his things. He lost texts, notes, and binders, which he had to replace. One prize week he lost five ball point pens and two pairs of safety goggles. He was terrified of the sophisticated laboratory equipment which he was required to work with.

He spent days surrounded by swarms of people, not one of whom exchanged a single sentence with him. His nights were troubled with dreams of Albert Rose. Again and again he wakened, thinking he had heard Joey scream. He was numb with homesickness. He carried a note he had received from Chickadee in his pocket and read it and re-read it until it was a worn, grey rag.

Every second of his time was programmed. The Bayrocks never let him out of their sight except when he was actually in class or sleeping. Dick even appeared at the technical school to eat lunch with him. Sundays he went to the unfamiliar Salvation Army church with the family.

He considered running away, but no opportunity presented itself; and in any case, awed though he was by their preoccupation with time, there was no denying their good heart.

The time he looked forward to most was the hour before supper. The family buzzed about, exchanging news of the day's activities, played with the Welfare babies and watched television. Sometimes he, Ronnie, and Dick engaged in good-natured wrestling matches in the middle of the livingroom rug. If things became too boisterous Nellie broke it up by giving the first one she could corner a baby to tend.

One evening André was sitting in the kitchen spooning pablum into a baby while Nellie prepared supper.

"Heard from Father Pépin today," she said. "Wants to know how you're getting along."

"Yeah?" He snorted. "What you gonna tell him?"

"What do you think I should tell him?"

"Dunno."

"Got your courses up to snuff, haven't you?"

"Sure. Keeps me running like an old cow with the heel flies after her, but — "

"It's only the last week of October. You're *where* you're supposed to be *when* you're supposed to be without anybody prodding you any more. Keep your room, look after your clothes, do chores around the house—" She grinned at him as she stirred flour into the roaster for the gravy. "You tamed down that awful language, and learned to eat properly. I think you're doing all right."

He ducked his head in pleased confusion.

"But nobody talks to me," he muttered. "Nobody hardly, outside of the house."

"They never will. You have to learn to talk to them."

All right for you, maybe. You talk to the cat if there's nothing else around.

"There is one thing," Nellie said, frowning. "Father Pépin wants to know if you're going to Mass."

"Mass? Jeez!"

She studied him speculatively. "You've been shoved pretty hard this last couple of months, but, believe it or not the worst is over. I know what you were thinking. Run away, first chance you got." She laughed at the expression on his face. "Think I don't remember? When they first brought me to town . . . " She sobered suddenly. "But there comes a time when nobody holds your hand. I believe that time has come for you. How'd you like to be alone here Sunday mornings? Just keep an eye on the babies and—"

Two whole *hours*—Nobody yelling at me—Nobody teaching me—

"Yeah. Yeah!"

He treasured those Sunday mornings when he was alone in the quiet house.

Nobody gaping at me. *Nobody.* Not one sonofabitch in the world. Bugs me. Dunno why—Eyes—Gives me the jiggers.

White man's world, huh? Yeah, I can pass the courses in their school. I can even change the washers in their water taps, but I might just as well be a goddamn fly on the wall. They ain't *mean.* They don't give a damn. Look through me like I'm shit. No, not shit. Like I'm nothing.

Nellie says it ain't easy at first. Christ! If it's ever easy, is it *worth* it? Ah, hell, maybe all I need is a piece of ass. Nothing doing around here, that's for sure. If Rose beat the shit outta me for balling Dodie, Sam Bayrock'd geld me for *looking* at one of them girls.

But there's girls around NAIT—Heard that Symons guy in the class talking. Dolly something-or-other. Says she's—Well, hell! I ain't gonna find a girl. Not till I quit shuffling around with my eyes on the ground looking like I lost something.

That week both Dick and his mother came down with heavy 'flu colds. Dick missed classes, and Nellie went to bed leaving the family to shift for themselves. André had finished his morning's classes when he realized that he had made no lunch for himself, and nobody had done it for him. He was hungry. He decided to venture into the cafeteria.

He bought some sandwiches and a mug of coffee, carried it off to a corner table and sat down with it. Four boys from the Earth Resources course were sitting together at another table. He wanted to join them, but no one looked in his direction, and he didn't have the courage to do so uninvited. They were craning their necks toward Symons. From the expressions on their faces, he knew Symons was telling a dirty joke. At the punch line they threw themselves back in their chairs with great hoots of laughter.

A skinny girl moved about, gathering dishes and piling them into a cart. André hadn't looked at her until Symons called,

"Hey, Dolly! C'mere." He drew her close and whispered something in her ear. She went into a fit of body-contorting giggles, and squirmed from his grasp.

"Bill, you're awful!" she said, going back to her cart.

It's Dolores! Dolores Olson! Be damned. Wonder what happened to the business course? Musta tangled with Thorvald's wife.

The boys grinned at each other and exchanged winks. One of them caught sight of André. "Hi, Macgregor. How yah doing?" he said, flapping a casual hand as they rose and strolled out of the cafeteria.

Dolores followed the direction of his gaze. When she saw André, she froze. She went to drop an ash tray into the cart. It fell, clattering and rolling across the floor. She swooped down to retrieve it, and came up to André, abandoning her cart in the middle of the floor. Colour rose and receded in her face. "What're you doin' here?"

"Takin' a course. Thought you was goin' to a business school, or somethin'."

She made a wry face. "Have you been — home?"

"Nah. Maybe at Christmas."

She rolled her lip under her top teeth and looked at him from the corner of her eye. "Well, do me a favour, okay? Don't tell anybody up there that you saw me. If Daddy found out I was here — I just couldn't go back to that farm. Honestly, I'd *kill* myself."

"Okay. I never saw you."

"You promise?" she insisted.

"What's the big deal? I never —

"You *promise*?"

"Jeez! Leggo of me. I ain't tellin' anybody."

What the hell's eating her? What did Symons call her? Dolly. Yeah, Dolly. *That's* the one he was talking about. Claims she ain't even getting paid for it.

He had no time to think of Dolores or any other girl during November. The pressure of the approaching first-quarter exams kept him scrambling all day and studying far into the night.

He was surprised the first morning after the exams to be stopped by an instructor in the corridor.

"Macgregor! Thought you'd like to know you made it through your first quarter. That's the tough one."

"Shoulda. I worked like hell."

The instructor laughed. "You seem to be hacking it better than most of the young guys that come to us out of the far north. What's the secret?"

"Dunno."

"Where are you boarding?"

"Pretty nice people. The woman's Métis. Married to a white guy, y'know?"

"Oh? Wish we could find places like that for some of these other young fellows. Maybe they wouldn't be running off to the bush all the time because they're homesick." He grinned and added banteringly, "You better stay on the good side of that family."

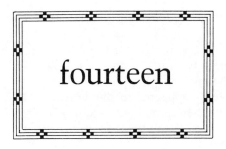

fourteen

André realized that the pressures on him were beginning to ease. It was not dramatic, or sudden; rather it was one small thing at a time. The city became a little less terrifying. He no longer felt as though he were being constantly watched. His fellow students sometimes included him when they went for coffee in the cafeteria. He became more sure of himself with the laboratory equipment. There were whole days when nobody corrected him for anything in the Bayrock household.

Christmas was fast approaching. When Nellie was not shopping, she was scrubbing and waxing floors or baking fancy cookies. Sam spent his spare time in the basement workroom refinishing an old walnut coffee table he had bought in a second hand shop. It was to be Nellie's Christmas present. André had hauled it downstairs for Sam when it was first brought home. Privately he thought it was a piece of junk that even Isaac would have disdained to buy at an auction.

One night he went down to the workroom to borrow a pair of pliers to pull a nail out of the sole of his shoe. Sam looked up from where he was replacing a piece of paper in the sander. "How do you like the table?"

"Holy cow! Dunno how you did it."

"Lotta work, but solid walnut's worth it."

"Smooth!"

"Wait'll I'm finished with the six hundred wet-dry. You'll be able to see your face in it."

André was studying in his room three days before the beginning of the Christmas holiday. He heard Sam answer the phone downstairs. Then Sam and Nellie were engaged in some sort of discussion.

"André, you going home for Christmas?" Sam called up to him.

"Yeah. Father Pépin sent me the bus ticket."

"But you'll be back before the New Year?"

"Gotta. Classes start — "

Sam and Nellie appeared in the doorway. "How would you feel about being left alone here to look after the place for three days?" Sam asked. "Folks want us all to come down to Calgary over New Year."

"Sure. Be fine."

"The babies are being adopted out before Christmas," Nellie said. "I'll leave you plenty to eat, and all you'll have to do is look after Stockings and the cat."

On the last day before the holiday the instructor for the mathematics class was late. Jimmy Bailey, sitting next to André at the table, was having difficulty. "What'd you come up with for an answer here, André?"

André shoved his work book down the table.

Jimmy compared his work with André's. "Ah, hell! There's where I went off the rails. You're a smart bastard, André." He leaned back in his chair and stretched until his tendons cracked. "Boy, will I be glad to get away from this drag for a few days, even if the folks did bugger up the New Year's Eve beer fight I was planning by deciding to stay home. What're you doing?"

"Lookin' after the cat and dog."

"Home?"

"My boardin' house. Folks goin' to Calgary."

"You mean you got a house all to yourself?"

"Well — yeah."

Jimmy snapped into an alert sitting position and examined André with bright hazel eyes. "What's that you're saying, man?"

"Now all I need's a girl friend." He meant it as a wry joke.

"Girl friend—! Man, we can scare you up a girl friend. We'll have the party at your place, and — "

Alarm stirred in André. "The folks I'm boardin' with'd never let — "

"Screw them! What they don't know won't hurt 'em." Before André could protest, Jimmy was on his feet calling out to the whole class, "Beer fight at André's New Year's Eve!" He glanced at André's text, got Bayrock's address, and scrawled it across the blackboard.

Jesuschrist! I gotta knock this on the head. But if I tell these guys 'no deal' now, they'll think I'm a bastard, and there's some of 'em just starting to treat me like I was human. No use asking Sam if it'd be all right. He don't allow beer in the house. I gotta *tell* these guys —

But he couldn't bring himself to his feet.

He fretted all that night as the Greyhound bus taking him homeward barrelled through the frozen woodlands.

That damn Jimmy! Well, it ain't his fault. It's mine for being such a gutless bastard. Anything in that house gets broke — Well, it just better not. That's all.

Dawn was breaking when the bus stopped in front of Dupée's hotel. It was snowing heavily. While three other passengers disembarked André stared out of the window across the frozen lake with its spruce-grown promontories receding wash by wash into the falling snow. A lump swelled in his throat.

Home! The bush — Jesuschrist! Forgot how much —

He had not slept in twenty-four hours. His senses still rocked with the motion of the all-night ride. When he got to the door of the bus he saw Rachel, Chickadee, and Isaac, shoulders hunched and hands deep in parka pockets, backed against the wall of the hotel. He stumbled down the steps. He and his family stared at each other across eight feet of muddy snow. Nobody spoke. Finally Chickadee dragged a small square package out of her pocket and grinned as she held it up for him to see.

Firecrackers! He giggled.

"Dere's moosemeat in du shack," Rachel muttered, "and new bread right outta du oven."

Once clear of the white man's part of town, Chickadee let the firecrackers go in a cannonade of noisy joy. From various Métis shacks children appeared, followed by sleepy adults. They yelled greetings, and made feeble, ironic jokes at André's expense. He was dizzy with the joy of homecoming. The Bayrocks, the Northern Alberta Institute of Technology, and the New Year's Eve party seemed as far away as Mars.

"What dey learn you, dis white man's school?" Isaac asked as they sat down to breakfast.

"Shit, mostly."

Isaac tittered. "Shit, huh? Guess you don't go dere no more."

André turned the wad of new bread over and over between his tongue and his teeth. It wouldn't go down.

"What you do dat place?" Rachel demanded.

He struggled for something that she might understand. "Stuff like measuring to see if light travels fastest through glass, or air, or water."

"Light travels? You crazy? Light just is."

"No, Ma, it—" The three of them watched him with puzzled, guarded expressions.

"Light travels?" Isaac tested it. Then he laughed in a helpless silent way. "Light travels, huh? Dat's shit for sure."

"You seen Gary One Blanket dat place?" Rachel asked.

"Ain't supposed to go in that part of town."

"Ain't supposed to? Who says? You liddle baby dat don' wipe his own nose?"

He looked down at his plate. "One Blanket—He's a bastard. I don't go with him no more."

There was a long silence.

"Métis ain't good enough for you no more, maybe," Isaac accused.

"Not Métis, it's — The time One Blanket swapped you the stolen rifle for half the moose carcass — You liked that three months in Fort Saskatchewan jail, there?" It was the wrong thing to say. He knew it even as he said it.

There was a chilly silence. Isaac rose from his place and dragged his chair over to the window. He hunched there, smoking and staring out into the snow. Rachel gathered up the remains of breakfast with an exaggerated clatter of pots and cutlery. Her lips were set in a sullen pout.

Stupid bastard and my goddamn mouth! First time I walk through the door —

He attempted to cover the moment by trying to coax Pee Dog out from under the bed. The animal crouched well out of reach, eyes glaring green mistrust, and lips snarling a warning.

"Guess he don't remember me."

Silence.

Chickadee sat beside the washstand painting her black-rimmed fingernails from a small bottle of scarlet enamel.

"Where's Simone?" André ventured.

"Johnny Crane," Rachel grunted.

The angry silence, filled with a thousand unsaid things filled the spaces between them again, and again André tried to break it. "How you gettin' along with Sister Bridget over at the school, Chicky? Grade eight this year, ain't it?"

"School? Think I'm crazy, too? They gonna drag me back there, they gotta catch me first."

Sore. The whole bunch—And it's my own damn fault. Well, I been belly-aching about missing the bush. I'm taking off—

Nobody looked at him as he put on his parka.

A wind was rising. The day had become much colder and he realized that he had left his mitts on the Greyhound bus. Before he had followed truck tracks a hundred yards into the spruce forest he was finding walking difficult. He needed his arms for balance, but with no mittens it was too cold to take his hands out of his pockets.

Stupid sonofabitch!

He stood for a little, staring at the tops of the spruce trees rocked by the whipping wind. It was cold. Cold. He hunched his body against it.

Can't stand here. Go see Alphonse, maybe.

Ernestine, Alphonse's mother, had company. Male, white, and solvent. She did not invite André into the shack.

"Alphonse? You don't hear du news? Justin Lacarrière, he dies. Marie — Nice house du government makes — Bathroom. Well. Lots of water. Nice cows—Everything. Alphonse, he sure makes dat place go. Cuts hole in du wall for water du cows in du bathtub dere. Real nice." She shook her head in admiration. "You still in dat Edmonton, dere? Guess you see dat Rose woman. Dey sayin' she's dat place now."

André removed one hand from his parka pocket and tenderly fingered his slightly crooked nose. "Ain't lookin' for her."

Ernestine giggled. "Might be next time Rose smash you nose he knocks it straight."

"Ernestine, for christsake come in, and shut that door," an irritated male voice protested from somewhere in the dark shadows inside the shack.

She grinned, and closed the door in André's face.

Now what? See Father Pépin, maybe. Just as well get it over with. Gotta see the old bastard before I go back, anyhow.

Early winter dusk had enveloped the town before he escaped the rectory. He plodded down the hill and along the lakeshore road with an cannonade of questions and exhortations still ringing in his ears.

No one was in the shack when he got there. The fire had been out for so long that the inside of the building was scarcely warmer than the blizzardy dusk outside. He lit the kerosene lamp and started a new fire. As he ate what remained of the reheated moose meat stew he looked about him and saw the shack through Nellie Bayrock's eyes.

Nothing was clean. Nothing was cared for. There were no curtains at the window. There was no privacy, and no way of achieving any. The rickety furniture had belonged to five different families, and was larded with the black grease of generations of filthy hands.

He knew Isaac and Rachel were in the beer parlour, but he was too weary to go hunting them. He tended the fire, hoping that Chickadee might appear. His eyes kept falling shut. Once he dozed off, and had to jerk himself into wakefulness.

At last he climbed into the bed where he and Joey had slept. The little boy's face, grinning trustfully, kept appearing behind his closed eyelids. The blankets were musty and unwashed. A bedbug attacked his ankle. He rubbed the itchy spot with the heel of his other foot.

He turned restlessly, unable to sleep.

Where the hell's Chickybird? They wouldn't let her in the beer parlour, and it's getting late. Suddenly he knew — Aubrey Sladden, or somebody like him.

Three days later, in the cold, clear sunlight of a winter morning, he boarded the bus for Edmonton. Only Father Pépin came to bid him good-bye.

His classmates at the technical school greeted him with back-slapping camaraderie. Plans for the New Year's party buzzed about his ears.

"Hey, man, like it's gonna be a bash." Jimmy Bailey crowed, "And wait'll you see the chick I got lined up for you, André, m'lad."

André forced a grin. He could not dispel a premonition of disaster.

The Bayrock family had already left when he returned from classes late that afternoon. He turned the key in the lock of the dark house and went in to be greeted by Stockings and the cat. He wandered from room to room.

Jeez! I wish I'd never opened my big mouth to Bailey and that bunch. S'pose I meet 'em at the door when they show up tonight and tell 'em, 'no deal'? Can't. They'd be sore as hell at me. Ah, hell! Ain't like Johnny Crane and Gary One Blanket was moving in for the night, but —

By nine o'clock no one had arrived.

Ain't coming. I can start breathing again.

Then Bill Symon's green Pontiac pulled into the drive. Bill, two classmates, and four girls climbed out. Cases of beer rattling, and wine bottles in hand, they came whooping up the walk. Symons began to chant.

"André Macgregor's the bastard
That is throwing a party."

Another car slammed into the driveway. Three more couples got out. They too took up the chant.

Bloody fools! Hollering like a pack of coyotes.

As the party trooped past him into the house, André saw the neighbours across the street come to their window and peer out.

They'll blab. Jesus! What'm I gonna tell Sam Bayrock?

Symons marched into the kitchen, yanked open the refrigerator, took out all the dishes of food Nellie Bayrock had left to last André for the holidays, and piled them helter-skelter in the sink. "Gotta have our beer cold. C'mon, you guys, pile 'em in here."

André had been so intent on what Symons was doing that he had scarcely glanced at the other members of the party.

"Hey, André," Jimmy Bailey called, "Your date — How's she for a doll? André, meet Dolly."

Dolores and André stared at each other, as Jimmy, backing out of the range of her vision, winked meaningfully at André.

How the hell did they manage to pick her? Some party this is gonna be.

"What's your problem?" Symons asked, looking at the expression on André's face. "It's a party. C'mon, jolly it up! Have a beer."

André stood on one side of the kitchen door, slouching against the jamb with a bottle of beer in his hand; Dolores leaned gawkily and ungracefully against the other jamb, not looking at him.

Someone set the stereo blaring. Two couples began to dance. Other couples necked in chairs. More shouting carloads kept arriving.

After a long time Dolores looked at André out of the corner of her eye and whispered, "You been up in the sticks?"

"Just come back."

"Suppose you told everybody you saw that I was working in the cafeteria at NAIT?"

"Never even thought about you, let alone talked about you. Forget it. Why don't you get a beer?"

She gulped off the beer, still standing against one side of the door while he stood against the other. People on their way for fresh liquor supplies brushed between them. They watched the party warm up, neither looking at the other.

"Want another one?" he asked when he saw that her bottle was empty.

"Yeah, sure. Why not?"

Wonder what'd happen if I put my arm around her. That dress is so short you can damn near see her ass. Nice legs —

When she had worked her way through most of the second bottle of beer, she asked, "You board here? Sure a neat house."

He grunted.

"They letting you have a party when they're away?" she probed. "Gee! I got a suite, but my landlady'd kill me — "

Oh, for christsakes, I don't wanna listen —

He summoned his courage, grabbed her around the waist, and swung her away from the doorjamb. There was no resistance in her body. She cuddled down beside him on the living room couch, a fresh bottle of beer in her hand and her feet curled beneath her.

The party was swinging. Bill Symons and another fellow were shouting at each other over some difference of opinion. The stereo was blasting. The floor bounced with the rhythm of the dancers. Jimmy Bailey swooped a girl up in his arms and disappeared upstairs into the Bayrocks' bedroom.

One of the dancers, a blonde in a long oriental caftan, stepped on the edge of her robe, lost her balance and fell over Dolores. Dolores squealed, shoved the blonde away, and climbed into André's lap, "Don't you let her get me," she said in an affected, little-girl lisp.

92

He tipped her head back and kissed her urgently. Instant response. He sought the nipple of her breast with quivering fingers. She nuzzled his face and nipped at the lobe of his ear. He could scarcely contain himself.

"We go find a bed, okay?"

"Ummm! C'mon." She pulled him to his feet.

He was suddenly aware that the front door was wide open. A blast of frigid air steamed into the room. Dancing stopped, although the music continued. Some of the guys shoved past, to join those already at the door.

"Get the hell outta here, O'Hagen," Billy Symons was shouting, "You buggered our last party!"

"You gonna put me out?"

André, heart booming and scalp prickling, abandoned Dolores and pawed his way through the crowd. Three burly strangers stood on the steps.

"Fuck off you guys. Dis ain't your party."

"Dis ain't, huh?" one of them mocked.

Fury boiled in André. He gave the fellow a shove that left him reeling for balance on the edge of the steps.

One of the three shoved André. He stumbled over Bill Symon's feet, lost his balance and fell across a TV tray. The tray collapsed and beer bottles rolled across the floor. A girl screamed. The music blared on unheeded.

By the time André had picked himself up O'Hagen had bulled his way into the middle of the room. But some of the Earth Resource party guarded the entrance from the two outside while the others closed in on the trapped invader.

O'Hagen grabbed a wine bottle from the floor, and suddenly it wasn't fun and games any more. But four boys landed on him before he could use it. They fell in a heap, arms and legs flying, with the coffee table underneath. Even through the shouts and curses and thud of punches André heard the crack and splinter of wood.

In seconds the Earth Resource boys had O'Hagen helpless. They carried him bodily to the door and fired him out into the snow.

The three invaders, yelling threats and insults, climbed into the car and roared away.

André scarcely heard the hubub about him. He stared at the

coffee table resting drunkenly against the couch, two of its legs broken, and its satiny walnut surface gouged and marred beyond even Sam Bayrock's ability to restore.

Jimmy, still puffing from the fight, patted him on the shoulder. "That's tough, André. We sure never thought — "

"Hell! Not like the roof's caved in," Bill said. "We'll pay for the damage."

André suddenly felt a little sick. "Look, guys — Maybe — I think you better go home now. Okay?"

"Go home! You sore at *us*? You threw the first punch. We never invited O'Hagen here."

"C'mon, you guys, let's split," Jake Quilley grunted. "Chip in for the damages and we'll go find a motel. Night's still young."

In minutes they were gone, taking their liquor with them. André gathered up the money scattered on the couch.

Eighteen bucks, pretty near. He sighed with relief. Sam's gonna be pretty sore, but anyhow, I can pay for what got busted.

The stereo still blared *The Guess Who*. He shut it off. The house was dreadfully still.

Something moved behind him. He sprang around. Dolores stood at the top of the stairs, frightened eyes staring at him out of a paper-white face.

"What the hell are you doin' here?"

"I hid in the bathroom when those guys started fighting." She leaned on the handrail and surveyed the room. "God! What a mess! We better get busy."

When they had picked up the beer bottles, dumped the ash trays and vacuumed the rug Dolores flopped into a chair, her rangy body collapsing like a gollywog. "Boy! Was I ever scared — "

"Yeah, well go find a bed someplace. I wanna get the lights out. If O'Hagen and them guys get real liquored up and come back — "

"Oooh!" She sprang to her feet and flew about turning out lights. "I'm not going to bed if you think — "

He snorted ruefully. "Well, the guys left us a coupla bottles of beer."

They sat silently in the dark house. Before André had finished his beer he knew that Dolores was asleep. He picked up an afghan from the end of the couch and threw it over her. It seemed a very long time until morning.

He wakened Dolores at six-thirty when he heard the first bus rumble by the corner. "That bus'll be back around the loop in ten minutes."

Before she opened the door to go out into the dark, she turned and slipped a scrap of paper into his hand. "There's my phone number if you want it."

fifteen

It was as black as a midnight cat as Dolores picked her way down the snow ruts in the middle of the road. Her feet, in cheap plastic slippers, ached with the bite of frost. She waited beside the snow-piled bus stop bench with her back to the wind, scrunching her toes to keep the circulation going. The bus pulled into the curb. Diesel fumes whipped around her. The driver watched her fumble for her bus pass, his expression speculative and sly.

So I've been out on an all-night party, buster. So what? Who cares what you think?

She scrunched low in her seat, holding her freezing feet over the hot air vents. She was the only passenger on the bus. They turned a corner and headed north into the wind down 109th Street. After several blocks, Dolores half lifted herself, clinging to the rail. She could see the roof of a neat, white bungalow.

What if I stopped in for breakfast with Thorvald and Sandra. She giggled. Wouldn't she be wild?

"After all we've done for that girl — "

Bitch!

Half an hour and two bus transfers later, she trotted down the dreary, poor-district street and around to the back of a shabby stucco bungalow. The porch light was off and she had difficulty fitting her key into the lock, but as she opened the door the light suddenly snapped on. The landlady, an ancient bathrobe hugged about her bulk, peered suspiciously down the steps. From behind her in the house the voices of many budgerigars filled the air.

"Happy New Year, Mrs. Sawchuck."

If I talk real nice to the old girl, maybe —

"Where you been?"

"Spent the night at my brother's place."

"Huh! Spend a lot of nights at your brother's place, don't you?" She retreated into her living quarters, throwing back over her shoulder, "Rent's due today."

Dolores made a face at the closed door and went down to her dingy rooms. She kicked off her wet slippers, removed the bedraggled party dress and tossed it across a chair. When she heard the landlady's heavy tread above her, she made an expansive gesture toward the dress, and, glancing up, mouthed, "There's your rent, sweetie. All forty-five dollars of it. It'll look real cute on you."

She opened the fridge and peered inside.

Nothing unless I spread that Crisco on some bread. Not even coffee. Hyaach! Go to bed. See if I can stop shivering.

She rolled herself into a ball on the narrow cot and pulled the blankets tight about her neck. But sleep eluded her. Her feet refused to warm. She turned flat on her back with her legs crossed, snuggling each foot under the opposite thigh, but the position was too uncomfortable. She rolled onto her side, pulled her knees up and snuggled her feet together.

Old lady's got the heat turned down. Saving a penny. Her stomach growled. Gee! Not even anything to eat at the lousy party. Yuck! Beer — I'm going to throw up.

She scrambled out of bed, rushed into the tiny bathroom and retched miserably.

Hope it's only beer. She wiped her eyes and peered at a calendar tacked to the wall. She counted the days. Nothing to worry about yet. Anyhow, the guys used rubbers, I think—I just *gotta* get the nerve to go to a doctor. Essie says once you got the Pill you don't have to worry no more. Wonder if she'd go with me?

She leaned over the sink, turned the cold water on, and drank with her mouth over the tap.

The shrill chattering of the budgerigars filled the house as Mrs. Sawchuck tromped into the room above the suite which had been converted into an aviary.

Dolores winced. Wow! Is she gonna start?

"Bobby's a pretty boy!" the old lady's voice boomed. There was a second's pause while she waited for the bird's response, then, "Bobby's a pretty boy!"

Oh, god! Not this morning — Dolores went back to bed, and

buried her head under the pillows. But it came through a hundred times, two hundred times, "Bobby's a pretty boy! Bobby's a pretty boy!"

Fifty budgies with a Ukranian accent! She giggled.

The voice still continued as she drifted toward sleep.

She wakened at three o'clock that afternoon ravenously hungry. A bit of sunlight the colour of diluted lemon juice quivered on the flowers on the wall paper. Dolores moved cautiously.

Soon as she hears me she'll be down for her rent. Dunno what I'll say. Week late last month and she gave me hell. She might throw me out. I *gotta* see Essie. The department stores'll be open tomorrow and we aren't working.

After she had washed and pulled on a shabby sweater and a pair of jeans, she wandered from one high window to another trying to see outside. Even stretched on tiptoe she could not see beyond the bank of dirty snow piled half-way up the panes.

She checked the pockets of her coat and her cheap plastic purse.

Fifty-seven cents and a bus pass — If I go just about supper time maybe Essie'll ask me to stay. Her old lady's not crazy about me, but —

She went to the bathroom and applied make-up, then stood back ruefully studying the results.

Dunno how Essie does it. She can make me look different every time. All I can do is —

She put on her parka, then her boots, noting with chagrin that the heels were already worn. She dreaded the cold outside, and dreaded the reception she would get from Essie's mother. She dawdled about the suite watching the clock until the hands reached half-past five.

It was a bitter day outside, with a north-west wind harrying sand-like snow across the streets. She caught a bus and disembarked a dozen blocks further north. It was pitch dark as she made her way down the snow-clogged, deserted street to the house where Essie lived. The house was in darkness, the curtains drawn, but she climbed the steps and rang the doorbell repeatedly. The only response was the frenzied yapping of a dog. She gave up at last and plodded down the street again to catch another bus, sheltering her frost-chilled windward cheek and her nose with a mittened hand.

New Year's Day. All by myself. And hungry.

Tears welled in her eyes.

Back in the district where she had her rooms, she went into a dreary, greasy-spoon café. It was empty except for three high school boys playing a juke box and a bored young Chinese who demanded, "Whaddya want?" before she had found a booth. She checked the prices on the catsup-smeared menu, then ordered a hotdog and a cup of coffee. She had three cents in her pocket when she left the café.

She sneaked down into the draughty, uncomfortable rooms. If I start cleaning up she'll hear me. Damn rent! Why didn't I —? Golly! Hundred and twenty dollars from the little jobs Essie and I did last month, besides my wages at the cafeteria — What'd I *do* with it?

Essie says I'm stupid with the guys; she's not giving anything away. But—"Ten dollars, or don't belly-ache to me about your lover's nuts"? I'd never have the nerve! Anyhow, I want it. Worse than the guys.

She picked up a dog-eared movie magazine and thumbed through it. There was an article promising the exposé of a scandal between two leading stars. She tried to read it, mouthing each word. She lost the thread before she had finished a page. With a sigh, she laid the magazine aside and crept into bed. She lay very still, trying to follow a situation comedy that was playing on Mrs. Sawchuck's television upstairs.

Gee! If I had a TV — She wiggled in anticipation. Maybe — Maybe if Essie and me do good next month.

Breakfast was three crusts of bread larded with Crisco. She was sneaking out of the house when Mrs. Sawchuck caught her.

"Where's my rent?"

"Bank'll open at — "

"Bank? Hah! Get that money by suppertime, or you're out." She disappeared into her living quarters and slammed the door.

Tears spilled down Dolores' cheeks as she struggled down the street to the bus stop. When she arrived on the doorstep, Essie's fat mother, her hair in curlers and a coffee mug in her hand, opened the door. "Oh, you—Essie ain't up."

"I — I gotta see — It's important — "

The woman sniffed, then muttering, "Oh, for godsake — " under her breath, went to the top of the basement stairs and bellowed, "Essie! That Dolores is here."

"Ohhh!" Essie groaned from somewhere below, "Okay. Send her down."

Essie rolled over in bed, her acne-scarred face puffy from sleep and her expression anything but welcoming. She blinked at Dolores. "What's up?"

"Department stores are open today."

Essie reached for a pack of cigarettes and sniffed, "You broke again?"

"Kinda."

Essie sighed, then said speculatively, "Be a good day, all right. Lot of people buzzing around exchanging Christmas presents yet, and the clerks not too bright after New Year's — Yeah."

"What're we waiting for?"

Essie examined her ironically. "For the stores to get good and crowded this afternoon." She sat up, lit a cigarette with an expensive butane lighter and groaned, "Ohhh! I gotta get a cup of coffee into me." She hesitated. "You have breakfast?"

"N — No."

"My old lady's gonna love this. Bitched at me all day yesterday, 'How you payin' for them fancy clothes? Some New Year's Eve party, comin' home at six in the morning.' Boy! I'd like to blow this dump."

The two of them hung about until early afternoon. Then Essie took charge, in the crisp, business-like way that Dolores admired as much as she resented.

"Today, you're gonna be yourself. Scrub all that gunk off your face and make two straight braids outta your hair, then I'll paint one of your front teeth to make it look like it was broke in half."

"Essie — !"

"Don't argue. Remember, chip this stuff off your tooth with your fingernail, and slip the elastics off your braids the second you get a chance.

"What am I gonna wear?"

"What you got on." Essie was dressing herself in a pair of plain, navy blue ski pants and a parka of the type that half the young women from the poorer working classes wore in Edmonton.

"Today your kid sister stole all the money outta your purse and you're gonna kill her when you get home," she told Dolores.

"You can hop a bus any time. I'll see you in the ladies' wear in the Southgate Woodward's at three o'clock."

She examined Dolores, who was standing fully dressed for the outdoors. "Jeez! Red mitts and a HAVE A NICE DAY button! Don't wear anything that makes it easy for somebody to describe you." She yanked the button off Dolores' coat, then rummaged through a drawer and brought out a pair of plain black mittens. "Get goin'. I'll take the next bus."

"Can you lend me some money? Just to buy bait? I'm kinda — "

Essie scowled, then extracted five one dollar bills from her purse. "That'll come outta your share of the take."

"You only gave me thirty last time!"

Essie laughed harshly. "Expect me to split fifty-fifty with you? It's *me* that takes the risk."

"Well, gee — !"

"Dolores, I wanna get this over with."

In the big store, Dolores rubbed shoulders with busy women shoppers, terror and excitement mounting in her deliciously. Then Essie brushed past her, without the slightest flicker of recognition.

Dolores selected a pair of panties from a display and approached the cashier's desk, the package in one hand, and two one dollar bills in the other. She drifted around to the left hand side of the desk and waited until Essie moved in, pretending to examine a coat on the right.

Dolores came up to the desk, her heart slamming her ribs and her breathing unsteady. She handed the cashier the package and the money at the same time.

The woman rang up the purchase so that the cash drawer snapped open before she looked at the money Dolores had given her. "That's two dollars and forty-nine cents, dear." She pointed to the price tag.

"Two dollars and *forty-nine*? Oh!" She opened her purse and stared into it. "My wallet's gone!"

The startled clerk gaped at her. "Perhaps you didn't bring it with — "

"I had it. Right here!" She thrust the open purse under the cashier's nose and shook it violently. "Right here. Look!" As she had planned, several coins bounced out, some falling on the counter, and some bouncing over it under the cashier's feet.

The woman bent to retrieve the coins, her back to the open till. Essie calmly reached across and lifted all the twenty dollar bills out of the till while Dolores pounded both fists on the counter, burst into tears, and yelled hysterically, "That sister of mine! Can't trust her — Wait'll I get her. Gimme my money back. Can't afford anything, now — "

Still weeping, she swung away at a rapid walk while the cashier stared after her. She ducked through throngs of shoppers, surreptitiously slipping the elastics from her braids and chipping the bit of black stage enamel from her front tooth. Outside, she dashed between hundreds of cars in the parking lot and neatly arrived just in time to board a north-bound bus on 111th Street.

She was still quivering with excitement when she unlocked the door of her rooms and went in to wait for Essie. She could scarcely contain herself, longing to recount every moment of the afternoon.

But when she arrived Essie was all business. "There's your take," she said, laying four twenties on the worn arborite table, "and I'll throw in the five you borrowed."

"How much did you — ?"

"Never mind."

Dolores swallowed her resentment in her desire to talk over the adventure. "Gee! I'll never forget that cashier's face — "

"Yeah. Well, I'm in a hurry," Essie said indifferently, heading for the door.

"When are we gonna try it again?"

"I dunno. Maybe never."

"Never? But it's so easy. And I kinda want a TV. Awful, cooped up here all week. Guys don't date, except on weekends — "

Essie looked at her from under her eyebrows and laughed nastily. "That's what you call it, huh? Dating."

Dolores felt her face redden. "How do you know but what — Well, guys get married." Her voice quivered with hurt.

"Don't hold your breath, baby. But I sure wouldn't let 'em lay me. Not without payin' for it."

"Essie — "

"'For christsakes use your head."

Bitch! I hate her. But one more night alone here, an I'm gonna —

"I'll fix us some supper if you want, Essie. Just gotta go to the grocery — "

"Nah. A guy's pickin' me up at eight."

"When we gonna work a department store again?"

"We better cool it."

"But I want a TV."

Essie considered, picking her teeth with her thumbnail. "Well, I could use a little extra right now, too. Sometime in the next couple of weeks. But that's it, baby. We're pushin' our luck. And I don't want you comin' around to the house no more, either."

"I don't want you comin' around to the house no more, either," Dolores mouthed at the closed door. Who does she think she is?

She started violently when Mrs. Sawchuck knocked on the door.

By six o'clock Dolores had shopped for groceries, eaten her supper, washed the few chipped dishes, and put them back in the cupboard. It was too cold to venture outside again. The evening, with nothing to do, stretched interminably before her.

Gee! If only a guy'd phone. Any guy. Even that André. Better than sitting here by myself.

She lay on the cot and stretched languorously.

Wonder how he is in bed? If it wasn't for that stupid fight on New Year's Eve — She giggled. Couldn't be as bad as that Jake Quilley. Shaking like his Mama was gonna come in and catch us —

Boy! Just wait'll I get married. Any time I want it. Essie, talking like no guy's gonna — I'll show her. First guy that asks me. Nothing I'd like better than to wave a wedding ring under her nose.

Mrs. Sawchuck was clomping around overhead. She went out at last, banging the door resoundingly behind her.

Gone to play bingo. Rent money's burning a hole in her pocket.

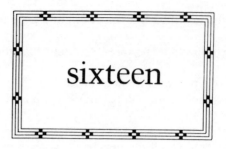

sixteen

André crawled into bed after Dolores left the house that New Year's morning. Stocking wakened him at noon, demanding to be let out. When he had tended to the cat and dog he went to look in the living room.

Not bad. Except for that goddamn table. Wonder how much — ? Well, even if I gotta take fifteen out of the bank to throw in with what the guys left — Table like that? Dunno. Twenty-five, maybe.

Clean up good today. Stores be open tomorrow. Have everything in great shape before Bayrocks show up.

All New Year's day he worked with vacuum cleaner, scrub pail, and wax. He gathered all the wine and beer bottles, dumped them into green plastic bags and stood them out beside the garbage pails, then shovelled the walks and the driveway down to bare cement. He was on his way downtown before the stores opened the next morning.

At five o'clock he returned to the house, dumbfounded and badly frightened. Musta been in half the damn stores in Edmonton. Table for thirty bucks? Fifty-seven they wanted for that one I thought might do. But it wasn't even wood. Jesus!

Them sonsabitches from NAIT — eighteen lousy bucks! They musta known — Yeah! Had me figured for a sucker, and they were right. Dunno what Sam Bayrock's gonna —

Car doors slammed outside, and the Bayrock family, noisy with good cheer, mounted the front steps.

"Happy New Year, André!" Nellie called as she opened the door. She stopped, eyes widening at the expression on his face. "What's the matter with you?"

He gulped and tried to say something, but his sticky tongue refused to work.

Sam shoved into the house. "What's wrong?"

André gestured toward the table. "Some guys come here, and — "

Sam was across the rug in three long strides. He stared at the table.

"And what else?" His voice was as calm and cold as the night outside.

"N — Nothin'."

"What happened?"

"Just some guys that are on the course with me — Never thought anything'd — "

"You had a party laid on here the second our backs were turned?"

"Well, the guys just kinda— " He shrugged miserably. "Been okay, but that O'Hagen — "

"O'Hagen!" Dick exclaimed. "He's a bad egg. Always — "

"Keep out of this," Sam snapped. He turned back to André. "Well — ?"

"Well, O'Hagen, he — well, he kinda shoved in on du party, y'know? And us guys piled on him, and—well, du table, y'know—?"

Jesuschrist! Sound just like the old man —

"I'll pay for — Soon as — "

"So, we can't trust you, eh? Four months we've been wet-nursing you, and you haven't learned a bloody thing!"

"Hold on, Sam," Nellie broke in. "Remember when I was a kid working for the Grayspears? The old Ford the judge let me drive, hauling kids, getting groceries and so on—? And the church picnic, and I let Johnson drive it? I knew Johnson wasn't a good driver, but — Anything to be one of the gang, so I — "

"So we should pat this character on the head and tell him it's all right to let a bunch of fools make a jack-ass outta *him*? Not to mention busting the furniture in our house?"

"Make him pay for it. I had to pay for the judge's car. Teach him to refinish — "

"Oh, for godsake—!" Sam snatched up a suitcase and headed upstairs.

André allowed himself a deep breath. Nellie had won him a

reprieve. Then he remembered that Jimmy Bailey and his date had been in the Bayrock's bedroom the night of the party. He hadn't thought of it until that moment.

Sam erupted through the bedroom door. "That does it! Our bed, a whore's nest! *Our bed!*" He thundered down the stairs and stood over André, who threw up his arm to protect his face.

"What'd André do?" Donna gasped.

"Never mind. You kids get out to the car!" Sam roared.

Dick, Ronnie and the two girls complied with amazing speed. Nellie backed toward the door, her face suddenly very white.

Sam advanced on André. His eyes narrowed dangerously. "All right. There's boxes in the garage. Get your junk together then call a cab. I'm taking the family out for supper. You be gone when we get back."

"Oh, Sam, not tonight," Nellie protested. "Where's he supposed—"

"*I don't give a damn!* Hand him his board back, then it's his problem."

Half an hour later André stood at the front window watching for a taxi. The cardboard boxes containing all his possessions were piled on the front porch. He sighed with relief when a cab rounded the curve and pulled into the driveway. He helped the cabbie load the boxes into the trunk, then hesitated on the sidewalk looking back at the house.

"Where to?"

He climbed in beside the driver. It was the first time he had been in a taxi. "Dunno."

"Well, you better figure it out. This is costing you money." He set the meter clicking. "You have got money, haven't you?"

"Yeah."

"Well?"

"Bus depot, I guess."

Yah! Bus depot. That's it. Fish Lake. Work for Mason. Get a trap line—Welfare, even—What the hell? Tell Father Pépin to go screw himself. Wasn't for him I wouldn't be—

But when he arrived at the bus depot the ticket clerk informed him that there was a severe blizzard blowing in Northern Alberta. All buses were cancelled.

What the fuck am I gonna do? Can't leave my stuff here. Somebody'll steal it. Can't pack it—

He sidled over to a chair, piled his boxes around his feet and sat there.

The security guard accosted him.

"Fish Lake? Might be a couple of days until they get that road plowed out."

"Well, my stuff — ?"

"Buy a ticket and check it through. Or there's lockers over there against the wall." The guard strolled away.

"Check it? Dunno what he meant. And for all I know, *any* key'll open one of them lockers. Jeez! If I knew the phone numbers of some of the guys from NAIT —

Another fifteen minutes passed. The guard was eyeing him narrowly. "Look, fella, I'm not telling you again, you can't hang around here."

The sonofabitch! What am I gonna do?

Hey! That Dolores — Gave me her phone number!

Feverishly he went through his pockets until he found the scrap of paper.

Her voice on the phone was more high-pitched and childish than he remembered. "You stay *here?*" There was a long pause.

"I ain't broke. I could — "

She interrupted with a long peal of laughter.

"I'll sleep on the couch. Anyplace — "

"All I got is a table, a couple of kitchen chairs. And there's a cot in my bedroom."

"Well, the floor even. Be okay — Just a coupla days — "

There was another long pause. Finally she tittered. "Old lady Sawchuck's out playing bingo. You better make it snappy."

She met him at the door. "Quick! Get your stuff downstairs. Can't count on the old girl staying at the bingo game if she has bad luck."

André ran back and forth with boxes and piled them, one on top of the other in the tiny kitchen. When he had paid the cabbie, he closed the door and looked about the apartment.

Jeez! Bayrocks' was a palace compared to this. Can't turn around —

A door opened somewhere above.

"There she is," Dolores whispered. "You made it just in time. Boy! If she knew I had a guy here — "

"Well, how'm I gonna get out when — "

"I'll think of something. Did you have supper?"

The TV upstairs blasted forth with an ad for Comet Cleanser.

"No, I —"

"Got a new jar of peanut butter, and there's bread in that drawer. I'll set the heat under the coffee."

While he ate she sat across from him sipping coffee and asking him about the events following the party.

"So, that's it," he concluded his story. "My own damn fault. I should have known them guys were usin' me for a sucker."

"I know how you feel. I remember how I felt when Sandra and Thorvald —" She broke off, winking back tears.

"Yeah, you was gonna take a—secretary's course, wasn't it?"

"Yeah, but that Sandra —" She sniffed.

"Kicked you out, huh?"

"Kinda."

They were silent in a bond of unspoken sympathy.

"But they don't know where I am," she said vehemently. "Daddy neither. I'm doin' all right. And I'm not goin' back to that farm. Ever."

Lots of guts. Gotta give her credit. Jeez! Maybe I'm stupid. Heading for the bush the first time things get rough. Glad I never told her —

She was examining a long run in her panty hose. "What'll you Earth Resources guys do when the course is finished?"

"Finished? Hell, that's forty years —"

"Whaddya mean? Jake Quilley says there's only a year and a half to go. And the worst part's over."

"Yeah, but —"

Shit! Gonna feel stupid telling her I'm quitting.

"But what kind of jobs can you get?" Dolores persisted.

He shrugged. "Well, they're sayin' seismic crews — Water drillin'. Minin' — Workin' up at the Athabasca tar sands —"

"Gee! You must be excited."

He giggled with embarrassment.

"You're sure a lucky guy."

"Oh, they're doin' a lot of mouthin' off, but I'll believe it when I see it."

"You'll see it." She grinned at him impishly. "You gonna take me for a ride when you get your first new car?"

"Ride? Dolly, I'm goin' to let you drive it."

You stupid sonofabitch! How can you tell her you're heading for the bush after a crack like that?

After a long silence, she asked, "What are you, André?"

"What am I?"

"Well, you know — English, Irish, Norwegian?"

He gaped at her. "You know goddamn well I'm Métis."

"Métis?" There was no doubt her surprise was genuine. "I never knew. You don't look — "

"You musta seen Ma and the old man."

"If I did, I didn't know. Daddy never let us kids go to town alone, or stay at anybody's place. Only visited relatives." She laughed sourly. "Funny. I lived in Fish Lake all my life, but I don't *know* anybody. At school, I was that queer Olson kid." She bit her lip, her face colouring. "First time I saw you was at Mason's garage last summer. And I sure never knew you were Métis." She frowned in thought, "So you musta gone to Separate School?"

"Yeah."

"That's funny. Daddy says none of the Métis ever get past grade nine, let alone — "

"Father Pépin's shovin' me, and payin' the shot."

"No kidding? Wow!"

Was paying the shot. Dunno what he's gonna say when he finds out Bayrocks kicked me out. Well, worry about that when I have to. Right now — Jeez! I'd like to get her into bed.

Mrs. Sawchuck shut the TV off at ten-thirty. Dolores and André stared at each other while the old lady tromped from room to room above their heads. The aviary door above the suite opened. There was a click as the light snapped on, then a cacaphony of squeals, squawks, and flapping wings.

"What the hell — ?"

"Budgies. Hey, that's it!"

"Huh?"

"How I'll get you in and out. She's nuts about the stupid things. I can always make an excuse for borrowing a pin or something in the morning, so that gets her out of the way while you take off, and in the afternoon, I'm gonna buy a budgie. Only I *can't* make up my mind which one. See?"

"Jeez! That's pretty good."

Her green eyes glinted with laughter. "I think so too."

Humming to herself, she drifted off into the bathroom. There was the rushing sound of the shower. When she opened the bathroom door she was wearing a long pink nylon nightdress with a provocatively revealing lace inset. He caught a whiff of perfume as she came up to him and began toying with the hair at the nape of his neck. Consumed in a flame of woman-hunger, he swooped her up and carried her into the bedroom.

"Jeez!" he muttered, flinging himself back onto the narrow cot beside her when they had finished. "My goddamn bones have turned to water."

She patted his belly. "Good, huh?"

"Good? I *guess!*"

She makes Dodie Rose look like a raw amateur.

She snuggled up to him and giggled. "Boy! If Daddy could see me now. He hates breeds. Get him started on that and he'll— "

"Yeah? Well, I don't want him trompin' the guts outta me."

"Honey, he'd tromp the guts out of *me* too, but he'd have to find me first."

Dolores did not go to work the next morning, and any thought of catching a bus had gone from André's mind. While a blizzard howled through the streets outside they made glorious love, ate what there was to eat, and made love again.

"Wow! Isn't it — ?" Dolores stretched, clenching her teeth ecstatically. She giggled. "Just like being on your honeymoon."

"Wish I never had to go back to that dumb Earth Resources stuff. Wanna just stay here and— "

"Well, you're going. Tomorrow morning. And me to work."

"Ah, hell! Day after tomorrow."

"Tomorrow. I heard Jake and Bill say that if they miss more than one day— "

"Them sonsabitches!"

"Baby," she leaned over him and kissed him, "you're gonna show those guys. *We're* gonna— " She stretched out beside him, flat on her back, eyes glowing in the dim light. "Sometime you're gonna have a real good job, and— "

He laughed. "Father Pépin might get sore and cut off the money. Only good job'll be drivin' a truck— "

"Let him cut it off. There's ways. I can— " She broke off. He could feel the light rise and fall of her easy breath. She turned to him. "We'll do it, sweetie. No matter what." She cuddled against him, her face on his shoulder. "Gee! I'm sleepy. I just can't—" She was asleep before she had finished the sentence.

André lay awake while the early dusk piled shadows into the room. His shoulder supporting Dolores' head and the arm around her numbed and deadened, but he did not move. Tenderness seemed to flow through his blood. He brushed his face against her fine ash-blonde hair, and marvelled at the soft glow of the perfect skin of her shoulder.

My Dolly. Nuts about her. Clean outta my bloody head. Never get enough of her. And a white girl, too. Jesus! I ain't doing so bad.

seventeen

As André hurried along a corridor on his way to class the following morning, he heard Dick Bayrock call his name.

He stopped reluctantly.

Jeez! Dont wanna talk to him. Not his fault, but —

"Man! Glad I caught up to you," Dick puffed. "When you didn't show up for classes yesterday we were scared you'd— Dad and Mom were down in the 97th Street bars looking for you, and — "

"Lookin' for me? What're you talkin' about? Your dad threw me out."

"Oh, for gosh sakes, you ought to know Dad by now. Blows his stack, then he's sorry. Look, I'm in a heck of a rush, but — Well, Mom says if you want to come back to our place I can get the truck after classes tonight and pick up your stuff."

"Back? Well, Jeez — That's — But — Well, I got a place now, and — "

"Yeah? Well—" Dick was backing away, "Long as you know you can if you want."

Be damned! Never knew there was people like that.

He narrowly missed colliding with Jimmy Bailey at the doorway of the classroom.

"Oh! Hi, André. Uh — How'd you make out with the landlord?"

"Got kicked out."

"Jesus!"

André brushed past him, found an empty chair and tossed his books on a table. Jimmy followed. He stood by André's chair, rubbing the side of his nose with his thumb. "Uh — Guess us guys could scare up a little more money. If — uh, if — "

Bill Symons and Jake Quilley appeared. They spotted André and came over to him.

"André got the boot," Jimmy informed them.

"Ouch!" Quilley said. "Where you staying?"

"Guess I could go back to Bayrocks'. The old man's cooled down, but — " He shrugged. "There's a girl."

" Speaking of girls, we just came from the cafeteria," Symons said. "Dolly cornered us." He slid a key across the table to André. "Said she forgot to give you this, and I'm supposed to remind you to wait until the light goes on in the room where the old lady keeps the budgies—whatever that means."

"André, is that the girl? Dolly?" Jimmy Bailey asked.

"Yeah."

The three boys exchanged glances.

"Well, Dolly's fine for a one night stand," Jake Quilley said, sniggering nervously, "but—"

"Yeah?" André bristled. "Well, when I'm out on my ass in the cold she's the only one that — "

"That broad belongs in a cat house!" Bill snorted.

"Fuck off! She's the only one that's there to do anythin' for me when I need it."

"Okay! If you're satisfied I dunno what we're — "

At that moment the instructor entered the room and the three of them went to find places at another table.

For the next two weeks André was giddily happy. He went to classes, slashed through his work, and sneaked into the apartment at night. Dolores insisted that he study, but when he had finished they made marvellous love until they went to sleep at last in each other's arms. All worries about money, thoughts of the past, and plans for the future faded into the consuming joy of *now*.

It did not matter that his classmates were cool toward him. It never occurred to him that he should have given notice of a change of address to the office. He shoved Father Pépin and the next month's allowance out of his mind. He had Dolores. He could not think of her during the day when they were apart without a painfully sweet catch of the heart.

He was jolted into reality one afternoon when he was working in the laboratory by an abrupt summons to the general office.

"There is a rule that we have the address and phone number of every student enrolled here," the woman in the office told him tartly. "If you move we want to know about it, and it seems you have moved." She paused, pencil poised expectantly over a form.

"The address?" He was mortified to realize that he couldn't tell her. "I — I dunno. I could take you there."

She snorted. "You mean to tell me you don't know where you *live*? Well, you'd better find out, and the phone number, too. I want that information before class tomorrow morning. And there's someone waiting for you in the north cafeteria. A Roman Catholic priest."

"Father Pépin?"

She turned away and began slamming through file drawers without answering.

André backed out of the office, his scalp crawling with unease, dodged through throngs of students and made his way to the cafeteria. He spotted Father Pépin waiting in the corridor outside. He looked furious.

"What is this I 'ear?" the old priest barked.

"Father?"

"You 'ave been thrown out of your boarding 'ouse? You break the furniture and make a fool of yourself there? Then you do not go back when they are kind enough to ask you?"

Two passing girls, overhearing, turned their heads to look from the priest to André. Their eyes filled with glee, and they hid laughter behind piles of books as they moved on down the corridor.

André's ears burned. "Father—Maybe you should listen—"

"Listen! Where are you living?"

"I — Don't matter. It's a good place."

"A good place? What sort of a family? Is there a quiet place where you can study?"

"Oh — Oh, yeah."

"You will take me there. I will see for myself."

"I — I can't, Father."

"Can't?" A black frown creased his brow and his whiskers waggled with agitation. "If I pay the money, I see the place."

André did not notice Dolores until she slipped her hand through the crook of his arm with a proprietorial air.

"What's the matter, honey?" Then, looking at the priest, "Who's he?"

André hastily disposed of her arm as Father Pépin portentously demanded, "Who is *she?*"

"Dolores," André muttered, "Maybe you better leave me and
Father Pépin — "

"*Who is she?* " Father Pépin demanded once again.

"I'm his fiancée," Dolores said pertly. "What about it?"

There was a long silence. The priest, neck out-thrust, glared at
Dolores and André alternately. "Are you living with this girl?"

"Well, Father — We — "

"You are living in sin?"

"*Sin!*" Dolores said indignantly. "You should try it sometime. Then maybe you wouldn't be so — "

"Dolly!" André protested helplessly.

Father Pépin ignored her. His mouth pursed with disapproval.
He scowled at André. "You — Come now! I must get you out of
this — this — Find you a proper boarding house. You are not to
see this girl."

"Father, I can't. Dolores is — is — I can't."

"Can't? Are you telling me you love 'er?"

"I'll never leave her, Father. She's — I'll never leave her."

The old priest glowered, his face scarlet with chagrin. "Then
you will marry 'er. I will not 'ave — "

"*We* say when we get married, or *if* we get married," Dolores
said. "You're not telling us. I've taken that kind of bossy crap
from guys all my life, and I'm not taking it from you."

Father Pépin made a heroic attempt to control himself. "'As
André told you I am paying for the course 'e is taking here?"

"What's that got to do with you telling us we gotta get married?"

"I will not waste my money on 'im unless I approve of the way
'e lives."

"Waste your money? What're you talking about? He's doing
great, but him and me — That's none of your business."

Father Pépin was purple. A huge vein throbbed in his
forehead. "André! You allow this girl to speak like this to me,
your priest? Come. I will speak to you alone."

"You talk to him, you talk to me too," Dolores said.

André's knees were quivering. He looked helplessly from one
to the other.

"Come!" the priest commanded.

Dolores grabbed André's hand. "Not without me he's not."

"Father — " André implored.

The old priest's face blanched. He flung up his hands in a gesture of rage and frustration. "Then be a fool! Worse than a fool. But never will you get one cent from me. Ever again." He turned and marched away from them.

"Phooey! Who needs him?" Dolores said scornfully. "I'll put you through the course, baby. Don't worry about that." She kissed him full on the mouth as people brushed past them.

She broke away, fished in her pocket, and brought out two slender imitation-gold wedding rings. "Look what I got! We'll make it official as soon as we can. We're both eighteen, but I'm sick of sneakin' around that apartment, and these'll keep old lady Sawchuck off our backs."

She caught André's hand and forced one of the rings over his knuckle. "There! Now you hold on a minute, baby. I gotta talk to Essie a minute before we go home."

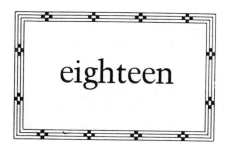

eighteen

André was shaken by Father Pépin's rejection — much more shaken than he wanted Dolores to know.

Gotta be crazy. Always hated the way the old bugger'd butt in and shove me around, but—Jeez! How'll I get along without—? Dolly's hot on me getting through this course. Well, if that's what she wants — Wonder what they pay her at the cafeteria? Never figured it'd be much. But she sure ain't broke.

A storm was blowing in, filling the school courtyards with sifting drifts of snow. While André waited for Dolores, he stared across the floodlit snow to the brilliant mosaic on the far wall of the building. When he let his eyes go into soft focus the mosaic reminded him of the beadwork his grandmother had done on the deerskin moccasins she used to sell. She had died long since, but he was swept by a sense of loss and nostalgia for her.

She knew what she was. An old breed woman. Wasn't trying to be nothing else. And nobody making her. Maybe—Maybe— he groped.

Dolores came loping along like a lanky boy. Her face was flushed, her green eyes shining. "Let's head for home before the storm gets worse. We gotta get groceries. And, boy! I can't wait to see old lady Sawchuck's face." She doubled up with glee. "We ought to just go down to the suite talkin' real loud. Soon as she hears a guy down there, she'll come roarin', and we'll shake the weddin' rings under her nose."

"Jeez, Dolly! I don't wanna."

"Why? Be a good joke."

"Nah. Let's get goin', huh? Got a hell of a pile of work — "

It was a bitter night with blowing snow riding a north-west

wind. André pulled his coat sleeves down to protect his mitten-less hands and shifted his pile of books from one hand to the other as he plodded beside Dolores through the snow-clogged streets.

At the back door they met Mrs. Sawchuck with a plastic garbage bag in her hand. At Dolores' introduction the old woman's eyes lingered speculatively on André and her lips compressed; then she shrugged, a wry smile pulling up one corner of her mouth. "Married, huh? Well, gotta give you a wedding present. Soon as I take this garbage — " She pushed past them into the snow.

Dolores and André stood in the back entry waiting for her to return. André felt foolish. He avoided looking at Dolores.

"Come in," Mrs. Sawchuck invited, squeezing past them and removing a pair of man's boots on the landing above.

They followed her through the house and into the spare bedroom above the suite. She turned on the light. The budgies in the cages standing about the perimeter of the room went into a flurry of flapping wings and squawks and screeches.

"This little fella— " the old woman said, going to a cage which held a single turquoise bird. "Guy bought him for his wife, only she don't like birds. I'll throw in the cage too, and enough food to do him for a week. You been saying how much you wanted a budgie, Dolores — now you got one, and he's a real sweetie. Just the right age, and I clipped his wings so he can't fly till they grow again. That way you can get him real tame in just a couple of days. Long as you don't scare him, nor tease him. They got a memory like an elephant. If you tickle the feathers under his chin he'll soon learn to like you, but don't touch his tail. They hate that."

André had never seen a budgie except once, briefly, as he passed through the pet department of Eaton's store. The sounds of their squawking above the suite had driven him almost to distraction when he had been trying to study. Now he stared at the little creature in the cage which Mrs. Sawchuck held out to him with mixed feelings of repugnance, pity, and fascination. The bird crouched on one of the bars, its terrified, round, black baby-eyes fixed on his face.

"He'll be a real jewel turquoise like his daddy, there." Mrs. Sawchuck pointed to a mangnificent specimen in one of the bigger cages.

118

"Gee! That's sure nice of you, Mrs. Sawchuck," Dolores said from the doorway where she stood. "But I dunno if we ought to take him. That's a pretty fancy wedding present — "

"I want him," André said, taking the cage from the old woman's hand. "Jeez, thanks! He supposed to stay in the cage?"

"Oh, no. More you let him out the better. Well, look here—" She opened the door of the large cage and the turquoise male that André had been admiring hopped onto her hand, walked up her arm, snuggled against her neck, and said so plainly that André's jaw dropped. "Sergie's a sweetie. Serge loves Olga."

"Jesus! He — He — "

"That one'll talk just as good if you wanna spend the time with him. Just like every other animal. Fastest road to his heart's through his belly. Give him a little nip of — oh, don't matter—Pear, banana, apple, anything like that every time you take him outta the cage and in two weeks, he'll be as tame as Serge, here."

"And talk?"

"Well, talkin' — That takes a while."

André backed toward the door with the bird cage in one hand, and a bag of feed in the other. He could hardly wait to get down to the suite and take the bird out of the cage.

Dolores followed, a sullen expression on her face. "What did you take that dumb bird for?" she snapped as soon as she closed the door behind her. "Bad enough, listenin' to the stupid things upstairs all the time."

"Never knew they was so cute." He set the cage on the table and grinned at the bird.

"Don't forget, we gotta get groceries."

"Oh, you go, okay? I wanna take him outta the cage. And don't forget some pears, or apples, or somethin'."

Dolores clicked her tongue with irritation and went out, slamming the door behind her.

When she returned fifteen minutes later, André had the baby budgie perched on one forefinger rotating its head ecstatically while he tenderly tickled the feathers around its chin and beside its ears.

"Look at the little bugger!" he chortled.

"Oh, for Pete's sake! Haven't you even got the coffee on?"

"I'm gonna call him Gabriel."

"What?"

"After Gabriel Dumont."

"Who's Gabriel Dumont?"

"Mightiest Métis of 'em all, wasn't he, Gaby?" He tried rubbing noses with the baby bird, which, after a brief moment of withdrawal, reached up and gave the flare of his nostril a gentle, tentative nip.

"Hey! See that? He likes me!"

"Oh, honey! Put that bird away, and let's get supper."

André complied reluctantly. He began setting the table while Dolores sliced an onion into a pan of hamburger.

Dolores giggled. "Boy! Wasn't old Father Pépin sore when I told him off this afternoon?"

André was suddenly irritated. "Maybe that wasn't so smart. Sure, I know he wants to brag how he put a Métis through school, and all that crap, but—" He paused, sorting and resorting a handful of mismatched cutlery. "I guess he thought he was doin' the right thing. And if you want us to get married, anyhow — Jeez! Why make the old guy sore?"

"Oh, brother!" She swung around on him, her eyes blazing with resentment. "If you think some old guy in skirts is gonna start tellin' us when to jump and how high, you got rocks in your head."

André could not bear her anger. "Dolly! Jeez, don't get sore, okay? I only meant — " he trailed off lamely.

After a moment she turned back to her cooking. André, setting the table, cast uneasy glances at her, but she did not speak until she began dividing the hamburger onto the two plates.

"Drain the spuds, André. I'm in a hurry. Gotta meet Essie tonight."

"Essie? What for? You seen her just before — "

"I *said* I gotta meet Essie tonight. Okay?"

"What're you gonna do?"

"Help her with a home perm!" she snapped irritably.

She ate rapidly and made no attempt at conversation. Before she had properly swallowed the last mouthful she was out of the suite, leaving him to stare at the dirty dishes.

He tidied the table and spread his books out on it.

Damn! I feel shitty. Dunno why, but —

He was still working at eleven o'clock that night with the

baby budgie cuddled between his shoulder and his neck when Dolores returned.

She was pale, but there was an air of triumph about her, and a glow of excitement in her eyes. She kissed him before she took her coat off. There was an unfamiliar cosmetic smell on her skin.

"Let's go to bed, baby, okay? Leave those books for tonight."

She started as she realized that the budgie was on his shoulder. "Damn bird! Put it back in the cage!"

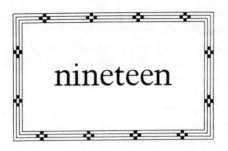

nineteen

Events moved rapidly the following week. During the Monday noon hour, Dolores dragged André downtown where they had blood tests taken at the provincial clinic. Friday, André cut classes. Accompanied by Essie, and another girl whose name André never did get straight, he and Dolores rode the bus down to the government buildings to have the marriage made official.

No Name had a head cold and blew her nose repeatedly during the dry little ceremony.

Essie looked from André to Dolores before she signed her name as a witness to the marriage and shook her head. "Boy! You two gotta be nuts."

"Best fourteen dollars I ever spent," Dolores cackled. "We ought to celebrate. I could stake us all to hamburgers."

No Name sniffed miserably. "Count me out. I'm going home to bed."

"Haven't got time," Essie sniffed. "Gotta go buy a new pair of shoes."

"Essie's jealous," Dolores said smugly, as she and André stood on the sidewalk watching the two girls walk off.

"Hell with her. Let's go have a couple of beers."

"Beer? Aw, honey, let's save the money. Anyhow, I got a real surprise for you tomorrow. And right now—" She giggled. "I can think of somethin' we can do at home."

At half-past eight that evening they agreed that they were hungry enough to get out of bed and prepare supper.

"You sure got good ideas, Dolly," André remarked, giving her behind a smack as she bent to hunt for a slipper under the bed. "Screwin' beats drinkin' beer any time."

After supper he went and got Gabriel Dumont out of the cage. The little bird hopped to his shoulder and began a busy exploration of his ear.

"Look, Dolly! He thinks he's cleaning my ears," he said through giggles of delight.

"Laugh if he bit you."

"Never bit me yet."

"Well, he bit me."

"Knows you don't like him."

Dolores sniffed. "You got studyin' to do?"

"Tonight? Jeez!"

"We gotta be outta here by noon tomorrow. Can't come back till supper time."

"Huh?"

"Somethin' to do with the surprise. So you gotta do your studyin' tonight."

"Gotta? Hell, Dolly —!"

"Tonight, baby."

Jesus H. Christ! Study when *she* says —

"We're gonna show 'em. Thorvald, and Daddy — Essie — And those guys at NAIT. You and me. We'll show 'em." She snuggled onto his lap. "You're doin' real good."

"Not bad I guess," he agreed, allowing himself to be wooed out of his rebellion. "Gettin' a kick out of the labs now, kinda. And that stuff we learn — Gotta work at it, but I can remember — "

She laughed and threw her arms around his neck. Then with a startled yelp she sprang to her feet frowning at a tiny, triangular wound on the inside of her arm. "Damn bird bit me again!"

"Jeez, Dolly, you scared him."

"I'll do worse than scare him if he keeps bitin' me."

André sighed and went to get his books. He had an essay due on Monday morning. English was not his strong point.

While he struggled with it Dolores sat on the other side of the table staring at him and biting her fingernails. The tiny snaps of her teeth seemed as loud as gun shots in the still room. Occasionally she started to talk. The third time she interrupted his train of thought with some inane remark, making him lose a sentence he had formulated before he could write it down, he hid his irritation behind a giggle and said, "There's some neat pictures in that geology book, Dolly. Why don't you look at 'em?"

"Well, gee! Can't I even talk to you? Sure is borin' — Just sittin' here watchin' a guy study."

"You're the one that wants me to. And I can't work and talk."

"Well, okay!" she said resentfully and flounced off into the bedroom.

But she was in a rare good mood when they got off the bus on Japser Avenue at one-thirty the following afternoon. They wandered along through the sunshine rubbing shoulders with strangers on the street and looking at displays in store windows. It was one of those days that come in late January when the air is soft with the false promise of spring, and the snow, reflecting the brilliant sun, makes the eyes smart with tears.

"Shall we go to a show?" Dolores asked.

"Show? Day like this, I wanna be in the bush."

"You're kidding!"

"Ain't there someplace where there's some trees, and not all them stinkin' cars?"

"Well, there's a park. Down by the parliament buildings," Dolores said reluctantly.

"Park, huh? Let's go."

They turned south toward the river, passing along the old, tree-lined streets that dropped down toward the legislative grounds. When they came around to the south side of the parliament building the sun, reflecting off the sandstone structure, was positively warm. But the building towering above made André uneasy. "Let's go down along the river."

"I'm not climbin' through snow."

"Well, the road down there — Looks like it's plowed out."

They skipped down the cement steps to the roadway below, and swung along it, shoulder to shoulder.

"Kinda nice, huh?" Dolores allowed.

Kinda nice? What they trying to do to these poor damn trees? Spruce ought to be left the way it grows. And them poplars — Jeez! Look like a guy that's had his arms chopped off and he's trying to grow some more in different spots. Only he ain't doing so good at it.

He was relieved when Dolores suggested that they go back

124

downtown and window shop until, as she put it, it was safe to go home.

When they arrived at the Sawchuck house Dolores glowed with excitement as she turned the key in the lock.

André stepped into the suite. The first thing he saw was a TV standing against the wall, looking as though it didn't quite belong. "Jeez!"

"It's only a second-hand black and white. But no more sittin' around here not knowin' what to do with myself at night while you study." She dropped to one knee and turned the switch, then looked up at him as she waited for the picture to come on. "Aren't you pleased?"

"I guess! But I dunno how I'm gonna study."

"You'll learn."

He was suddenly terribly uneasy. "Dolly—Them things cost a hell of a lot of money. How — "

"Baby! You gave me nearly a hundred and fifty when you moved in!" She sprang up and dug her fingers into his ribs, tickling him mercilessly. He was helpless. He doubled up and rolled on the floor.

"Cut it out! Cut it out!" he begged, capturing first one of her hands, then the other.

"How, sweetie? Don't you worry about *how*. It's there, isn't it? Now, relax and enjoy it while I fix us somethin' to eat."

twenty

The first weeks of February were wonderful for Dolores, in spite of the weather, which turned viciously cold and remained that way. She and André struggled back and forth between the suite and the technical school loaded with sweaters, parkas, overshoes, mittens, and scarves tied about their heads which left only slits of eyes exposed to the frost. Since she was country bred to hardship, it scarcely concerned her.

But other things did.

I *gotta* go to a doctor and get the Pill. Makes me squirmy, a doctor looking at my bum, but André hates rubbers. Really cook our goose if I got pregnant and couldn't work before he finished his course. Oh, but I don't know — That Mary Bettery up home — Wasn't on the Pill or anything else. Eight years before she had a kid. Nothing's gonna happen in just a couple of months, I don't think —

Gotta get André another pair of mitts. Second pair he's lost. Wish he'd learn to look after things. Sweater, slide rule — Costs money. And the *groceries* — I'm always hauling bags home, and there's never anything in the fridge.

Three bucks to last till pay day, and it's only the twenty-first —

Well, it's dumb! Spending my whole day off worrying about money. The stores'll be open tonight. Essie's been sore at me ever since I got married, but — Bet she's getting kinda broke. Hasn't been at work all week. Hope she's not sick, or something. I'll phone. No. Her mother might answer. I'll just go down there. Darn bus pass has run out, but there's no way I'm wasting fifty cents. I'll hike it. Won't kill me. I've been cold before.

Essie's mother didn't even invite her into the hallway. "Essie took off for Vancouver. Don't know where she's stayin'. She ain't wrote." She closed the door firmly, leaving Dolores shivering in the steel-grey cold.

She bit her lip. Tears pricked behind her eyes as she turned back down the street again.

Left? And never even told me — Can't play the department store game without a partner. Gosh! If André didn't *eat* so much —

She shuddered, muscles tense.

Wow! It's cold. And now I'm facing the wind. Better watch it, or I'll freeze my face. And that darn left foot — Toes are numb. I'll have to walk fast.

It was an eerie night, filled with floating frost crystals. A green glow hung over the city. Over each street lamp stood a towering shaft of light, but between lamp standard and lamp standard lay pools of murky shadow. Moaning softly to herself, Dolores passed from shadow to light to shadow again.

André was watching *Popcorn Playhouse* on television and sharing bits of a chocolate bar with Gabriel Dumont when she stumbled through the door. "Where you been? Jesus, Dolly! You froze your face."

"Foot, too. Help me with my boots."

The left foot was dead white, the toes faintly blue, when he took the boot off.

"Rub it with snow," she begged.

"Nothin' doin'. Better to put a person in a bath that ain't quite warm."

In the bathtub Dolores squirmed in agony while she thawed out. André dried her and found an old pair of flannelette pyjamas for her. Then, with two blankets wrapped around her, she huddled beside the hot air register, shuddering with recurrent chills. Her foot, both cheeks, and her nose were raised in glassy water blisters, and the flesh beneath was a dull, unhealthy red.

As André handed her a bowl of hot soup he asked, "Where were you, anyhow?"

"Essie's."

"Must like that broad better'n I do. Wouldn't freeze my ass to visit her."

Dolores hobbled into the bedroom without answering.

She was too sick to go to work the next morning. She slept off and on until early in the afternoon, then worry about having nothing to eat in the place drove her from the bed. She was delighted to see the heavy frost covering which had obscured the window for weeks beginning to melt away.

Warming up outside! Great! I'll get dressed and see if I can wear my boots again. Go down to the grocery and blow that three bucks on some Kraft Dinners, and — well, a package of oatmeal and some skim milk powder, I guess. Keep us eating. Maybe I can go to work tomorrow.

But before she had returned to the rooms with her groceries it was plain that she would be in no condition to go to work for some days still. The pressure of the boots was excruciating to the frost bites. For the next three days the rooms became her prison. She sat with her injured foot propped on a kitchen chair, stared at TV and fretted about money. She expected that André would begin complaining about the monotony of the food, but he didn't seem to notice.

After classes on Friday afternoon he bounced into the room. "Jeez, it's nice out. Must be — "

"Where's your overshoes?"

"Dunno. When I went back to get 'em they — "

"You mean you never put them in your locker?"

"Well — "

"Overshoes, text books, slide rules — ! What next?"

"Well, jeez! Ain't the first time I been without overshoes."

"And what if we get another cold snap?"

He blinked unhappily at the puddles melting off his shoes and did not answer.

She sighed. "Well, never mind. We don't have to go anywhere till Monday, and that's pay day. I'll be able to go to work then, and Tuesday's my day off. If we're lucky the good weather'll hold. Soon as I square up with old lady Sawchuck I'll go buy groceries, then head downtown and see what I can do about overshoes for you. Size ten, isn't it?"

Mrs. Sawchuck hiked the rent by ten dollars. The price of groceries had gone up, so that even after the most careful selection, Dolores was left with scarcely enough money to buy a pair of toe rubbers.

Cold stony broke till the next pay cheque? Damn that Essie!

Well, I'll just go downtown and hang around. Something might turn up.

Something did turn up; when it did, Dolores considered it an amazing piece of luck.

It was late afternoon. She had hung about in one or the other of the three main department stores all day. She was weary from tension, and becoming very hungry.

Heck with it! I'll just go down to the bargain basement and buy André a pair of rubbers there then —

As she was passing through the fur department of the Hudson's Bay store, she saw a very well-dressed matron talking to a younger woman, obviously her daughter, whose attention was divided between the mother's words and her own two-year-old who was tired and exceedingly cranky.

The matron opened a morocco leather handbag and extracted a pack of cigarettes and lighter from it just as a clerk appeared carrying a gorgeous sapphire mink coat.

"Is this the shade you had in mind, Mrs. Sodderstrom?" the clerk asked, laying the coat across a counter. She blew into the fur. "Now, if you'll notice — "

The matron dropped the cigarettes back into the purse and rose to go to the counter, leaving the purse wide open on a chair. "What do you think, Bertha?" she asked her daughter.

The girl joined her to examine the fur at the counter, turning her back on her little boy.

Dolores put a rack of coats between the women and herself, looked around carefully, then made a threatening motion and a hideous face at the little child. He opened his mouth in a screech of terror, raced to his mother and buried his face in her skirt.

While the attention of the three women was on the child, Dolores — with a calm aplomb that made her wish Essie could see her — extracted the wallet from the matron's open purse and walked toward the womens' washroom. She went into a toilet compartment, closed the door behind her, and opened the wallet with quivering hands. She snatched the money out of it and shoved it into her pocket, pushed the wallet down out of sight in a receptacle for used sanitary pads, and walked out of the store.

When she had the suite door safely closed behind her she counted the money.

Oh, wow! Six hundred dollars, nearly! We're set. Oh, if I could only tell André — With what I'm making it'll carry us right through till summer. And if he gets a good summer job —

Only one thing bugging me — Yaa-ch! When I think of that little brat this afternoon — Well, it's dumb stewing about it. I'll phone for a doctor's appointment right now.

The receptionist's voice on the other end of the line was cool, and bored, "Yes, Mrs. Macgregor — Now, uh — The date of the onset of your last period?"

"Well — I'll have to check."

"Please do. I'll hold."

When Dolores returned to the phone, she tried to cover her dismay with a giggle. "Gee! I'm a week late, nearly. 'Course, it don't mean *anythin'*. I've — I've missed before."

But she couldn't believe it didn't mean anything. She could not confide her worry to André. There was a week of tense and irritable days before the appointment. Several times she and André nearly quarreled over petty things.

She arrived at the doctor's office an hour early. She was too worried by now to care about the embarrassment of being examined.

When the doctor had finished, he came around to the side of the examining table, took one of her hands between both of his, and said, "M'dear, the Pill is not for you. Not at this moment, anyhow. I judge you to be six or seven weeks pregnant."

Dolores snapped up to a sitting position. "Pregnant! You're nuts. I *can't* be."

"Well—of course we'll check the lab specimen, but I couldn't be more certain."

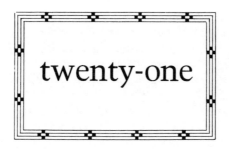

twenty-one

The sun warmed André's face as he started for home that night. Rivers of melted snow flowed along the curbs and gushed into the storm sewers. Spring's coming, he thought, coming sure as hell! He sighed joyfully and unbuttoned his coat. Don't seem like spring, though. Not here. Goddamn squared-off houses, and goddamn squared-off yards. Trees, yeah. But nothing growing around the feet.

Pussy willows in the bush pretty soon. Christ! Sometimes I want the bush so bad I can damn near taste it. Wonder what Ma and the old man'd be doing now? Long time since I heard from Chickadee.

Time they see Dolly, Ma, and the old man—I dunno. Maybe —Well, shit! She knows I'm Métis. What's so great about her old man? Or the old woman far as that goes?

That Thorvald — Never see him. And Dolly don't seem to care. Dunno about these white bastards. Suppose Simone was living somewhere in town—Maybe I ain't crazy about her, but I'd see her. Funny Dolly never sees Thorvald.

He lifted the heavy load of books from one hand to the other. Fucking books! Wanna puke every time I open the goddamn— Clock kicks me outta bed. Says when I go to school. Says when I go to bed. Says when I eat. Wonder it don't say when I ball Dolly.

He sighed. If it wasn't for Gabriel Dumont—Jeez! He's a cute little bugger. Says, "Goddamn you, André, gimme a kiss."

Dolly don't like him. But, jeez! Without Gaby, I dunno —
He opened the gate of the Sawchuck yard and plodded through

the heavy snow toward the back door. Two crows flew overhead, conversing raucously with each other.

Crows! Jeez! Spring for sure. I'm gonna get Dolly. Go to —
Don't matter. Park, river — Someplace —

He scampered down the stairs and flung into the suite. "Dolly? Let's — "

The bedroom door was closed. Muffled sobs came from beyond it. He opened the door and peered in. "Dolly? What's wrong?" She did not answer: His eyes were still recovering from the brilliant sunshine outside, and he could only just make out her form, a miserable heap with its face buried in a pillow.

"Dolly?" He sat on the bed and stared at her.

What's wrong with her now? Jeez! Howling like Pee Dog with his tail in a weasel trap. Sooner have her like Ma, or Simone — Throw things, swear — But they don't bawl.

His heart had been set on an hour in the sun. He was hard pressed to choke irritation. "Dolly! What's — "

With a spasmodic wrench, she flung herself against him, burying her face against his shoulder. "André, I'm — I'm pregnant."

He froze, not certain that he had heard. "You're — You're gonna have a kid?" He forced her away from his shoulder and looked into her face. She nodded, eyes closed. When he relaxed his hold she buried her face against him again.

"Who says?"

"Doctor."

Wave after wave of excitement swept over him. He shook Dolores, half in play, and half in irritation. "You bawlin'? Jeez! That's the greatest thing I ever heard."

He shoved her aside and capered about the room slamming his fist into his palm. "Gonna be a daddy! *Jesuschrist!*"

Dolores gaped at him in red-eyed consternation. "You crazy? What about your course? How'm I gonna — ?"

"Course? Fuck the course! Time I slam them glass doors behind me'll be the happiest — "

"And do what?"

"How the hell do I know? Don't matter."

She scrambled off the bed, caught her toe in a tangle of blankets, staggered, recovered herself, and faced him, her face flaming. "You will not! *You will not!*"

"Who says?"

132

"I say. You're gonna be somebody—"

"Somebody! Poor dumb sonofabitch with his balls tied to a clock. That's what you—"

"We could do it, André. So easy. If it wasn't for *this* —" She looked down with an expression of disgust at the caved-in flatness of her belly. "I can't believe it. Maybe the doctor's wrong. Maybe—" Suddenly, she froze, palms pressed to her belly. She straightened slowly, drawing breath through her open mouth, with her unblinking eyes fixed on his face. "I know! I know! That Bessy Chorney at NAIT—Y'know? The skinny one with the glasses? Abortion last fall. I'm gonna ask her—"

"Abortion? That's where they—?" He grabbed Dolores, fingers meeting bone in her upper arms. "Don't you say that no more, or maybe I'll break your goddamn neck."

"You're hurtin'! Leggo!" She backed off rubbing her arms. "*You'll* break my goddamn neck! Father Pépin talking'." She gestured toward her belly. "What do you care—?"

"I care. And it's *me* that's talkin'."

"You're crazy. You're *crazy*! We're okay for this year. Only a couple of months left on your course. But unless you get a decent job this summer—How can I work next year and look after a squallin' brat?"

"Ain't askin' you to. To hell with NAIT."

"Don't say that!"

"Dolly—"

"I won't stand for it." There was a hard, sly expression on her face. Her lips set and her eyes narrowed. "You want the kid?"

"Damn rights I want the kid."

"Okay. You finish the course. Otherwise—And don't give me crap about breakin' my neck."

André stood flexing his hands and staring helplessly at her.

They did not speak to each other for four days. After the last lab on Friday afternoon he went with some of the boys from class to drink beer in the Cromdale Hotel. He had a fuzzy memory of a fight with Bill Symons. He didn't know how he got home. He woke at noon with a split lip and a pounding headache. Dolores was crying in the kitchen. He buried his head under the pillow and went back to sleep.

It was late in the afternoon before he wakened again. He could hear Dolores in the shower. He turned flat on his back, linked his hands, and rested his head on the palms. His muscles were sore and the split lip made him wince when he opened his mouth.

Pretty dumb. Bumming beer off the guys, and picking a fight with Symons. Be sore at me again. Not so good. Gotta work with 'em. Should invite 'em down for beer on me Monday night. I'll take ten bucks offa Dolly now. Tell her when she's through in the bathroom. Keeps money here someplace. Seems like I seen her putting it into the bag where she keeps that face paint.

He padded across the floor, opened the top drawer of the bureau, and took out the make-up bag.

Twenty bucks all she's got? Too much. Take that to the beer parlour, and I'll blow it.

He opened her purse, which was hanging from the mirror support.

Two dollars, and some chicken feed. Buy beer with that, and it makes me look cheap. Better ask her to change the twenty.

He put the twenty dollar bill back in the make-up case and went to put it back in the drawer. He snuggled the case back where he had found it beside a pile of lingerie. As he did so he noticed the edge of a worn envelope sticking out from under the paper lining the drawer. Curiously, he pulled the envelope out.

Five hundred and—? *Jesuschrist!* How'd she—? He counted the money again, then carefully put the envelope back where he had found it. Alarm jangled in him. He let himself down on the bed and stared into middle distance while he did a rapid calculation.

Say she's earning two bucks an hour—Even with the money I threw in on the deal when I come — Rent, grub, TV, books, clothes — Jeez! There's no way!

His mouth was sticky, and his hands began to sweat.

Dolores appeared in the doorway. She looked dejected, sick, and utterly miserable. "Honey," she sniffled, "I can't stand it when you're mad at me."

"Don't start that bawlin'," he said irritably.

"But you're mad. Baby, it's just that I want you to be—I know you can. I *know* it."

"Yeah? Well, I'm gonna get cleaned up."

He was a long time in the bathroom. Confusing and contradictory thoughts tumbled through his mind.

134

No use stepping around it, he decided finally. I gotta find out.

When he had dressed and combed his hair, Dolores called him for supper. Ordinarily a beef steak was the treat of treats. Tonight he ate it without tasting it. He ignored Gabriel Dumont's frantic bids for attention.

He stirred sugar into his coffee. Well, here goes.

"I'm buyin' beer for the guys Monday night, Dolly."

"You're — ? We can't afford — "

"Not gettin' plastered again. Ten bucks'll do it. They're sore at me, and I gotta work with 'em."

"Look—We haven't got much more than that to do us till pay day."

"Dolly," he took a deep breath, and his muscles tensed, "where'd you get that pile of money you got cached in the drawer?"

The pupils of her eyes flared. "How'd you find — ?

"Where'd you get it?"

"Mama."

"How? You said your Ma never knew where you was."

"Well, you see, I wrote to Mary Bettery. She's the neighbour, y'know? And — "

"Dolly, you're lyin'."

She reddened, from the throat of her blouse to the roots of her hair. Her lips moved, but no words came.

"Where'd you get it?"

"Well, all right. There was this old rich biddy foolin' around with a mink coat in the Hudson's Bay. Lifted the wallet out of her purse. Never hurt her any, and — "

"How much?"

"Never spent anythin' except for your overshoes, and maybe thirty — "

"How'd you pay for the TV?"

"I *earned* — "

"Dolly, for christsakes! I ain't that dumb. If we squose a nickel till it hollered, all we'd do is pay rent and keep eatin' on your pay. Buy a TV? Even second hand? Shit!"

She burst into tears, hiding her crumpled face in her hands. "I did it for you."

He shoved himself away from the table, went into the bedroom and closed the door. For a long time he sat on the edge of the unmade bed, his hands trembling; all the while Dolores cried in the kitchen beyond.

She was a pitiful sight when she opened the door and sagged against it as though too weak to stand. "What're you gonna do?" "How the hell do I know? And quit that bloody bawlin'. Gives me a belly ache."

"André, I only did it for you."

Distractedly, he got up and began picking up various pieces of clothing that were scattered about.

"What are you gonna do, André? André, you're not leavin'? Honest to God, I couldn't stand it. I couldn't."

He turned to look at her, a pair of dirty socks dangling from one hand. "Think you're pretty smart, huh? Damn lucky, so far, that's all. *Damn* lucky. Sometime somebody's gonna—" With a sudden violent gesture he flung the socks on top of a pile of clothes.

"I'll never do it again, André. Honest to God, I'll never — "

"You better not, or by the Jesus Christ—! Seen enough of that crap with Ma and the old man. Goddamn Mounties always nosin' around — "

"André, please — I promise. Never — "

But he never really trusted her again. He was suspicious of every minute of her unaccounted time. He despised himself for it, but he calculated everything she bought against her pay cheque and the money in the envelope.

Like a goddamn screw in the jailhouse. And me — Waste money! Another text last week. Good thing my pecker's hung on tight, or I'd lose that too.

His discontent grew with the spring, which after a few minor setbacks, came with a rush. One week he went to classes wearing overshoes and a parka; the next, sneakers and shirt sleeves. There came an evening when he stopped to watch a flight of Canada geese high above the city, veeing north and ever north. They filled him with almost unbearable yearning.

Catkins and pussy willow. Frogs singing all night long. Mallards in the sloughs. Young moose and deer—Indian in me gets an itchy foot in spring. Like the rest of 'em. Ma and the old man —Long time since I seen 'em. Wonder what Dolly'll say when— Claims she don't know one Métis in Fish Lake from another.

Jeez! Suppose the kid turns out a black, ugly little bugger like the old man? Lot of white blood shows in me. Don't follow it's gonna show in the kid. Maybe Dolores don't like that —

Poor old Dolly. Sure ain't feeling good. Guess I ain't much help. Dunno—But ever since I found that money—Ain't so good balling her no more.

Gets sore as hell when I play with Gaby. Says she's sick of playing second fiddle to a stupid bird. Jeez! It's comical, the look on her face when Gaby cackles just like she does. I keep telling her he don't know what he's doing. Just imitates sounds, but she don't believe me. There's times I figure she'd like to wring his neck.

One morning he was called out of class and asked to report to the general office.

Hope it ain't Dolly real sick, he thought as he hurried along the sunny corridor. Musta felt pretty lousy or she wouldn'ta stayed home from work this morning.

When he entered the office, Isaac and Rachel were waiting for him, slumped in two chairs against the west wall, hand-rolled cigarettes plastered to their lower lips. The whole office was redolent with the dear, familiar smell of newly-tanned moose hide moccasins.

twenty-two

Dolores opened her eyes and forced them to focus on the face of the alarm clock, then squeezed them shut again.

Nearly noon—Ought to get up. Place is a mess, but—Oooh! If this is having a kid, somebody else can take the next turn. Can't even stand the smell of the newspaper. Coffee — Cigarette smoke! Her stomach rebelled at the thought. She sighed and dragged herself to a sitting position. Can't lay here. Gotta get some clothes to the laundromat and —

"Don't you bite me," Gabriel Dumont said cheekily from his cage.

"Shut up, you little beast!" She picked up a heavy sweater and flung it over the cage. "Not listenin' to you yap all day."

She wandered about the suite in an old night dress that was becoming tight across the belly.

I'm hungry. Starvin'. But I know if I eat I'm gonna puke. Ohhh! I'm goin' back to bed.

The baby stirred. She couldn't find a comfortable position.

Yeah, I know you're there. I'm not so crazy about you being there, but — Five months to go. Twenty-eighth of September, the doctor figures—I just can't think about it! The awful stories Mama used to tell about when us kids were born — Astrid! Suppose the kid's like—I couldn't stand it. Don't know what I'd do.

Terror swept through her. Maybe—Oh, God, no—She turned her face into the pillow and sobbed wildly, "I want Mama! I want Mama!"

The door opened. She swallowed tears and blew her nose. "André? Is that you?"

"Hey, Dolly, you still in bed? We got company."

"Company? Who?" She raised herself up onto her elbow and peered into the kitchen.

There, crowded behind André, were a couple she had often seen in Fish Lake. She couldn't have named them, but she had always thought of them as 'dirty Indians'. She had seen the woman poking with a stick through reeking garbage in the town dump. Once she had seen the man, drunk, and disgustingly sick at the back of the hotel. Now they examined her with opaque, black eyes set in heavy, expressionless faces. Her stomach nearly rebelled at the reek of their smoke-tanned moccasins. She yanked the blankets up to her chin to hide herself.

"Who — Who are they?"

"My folks."

"What?"

"Ma, and the old man."

"André, you — *Your folks?*"

"Yeah. Maybe you could get up and make a little coffee, huh?"

"Coffee! You know I can't *stand* coffee. Shut this door."

"Door? Oh, yeah. Sure."

She sat up, staring at the closed door.

His *folks!* Them? My God, if I'd known — I musta been crazy —

"Dolly," André called through the closed door, "we're outta tea. Anyhow, the folks'd sooner have beer. Me and the old man's gonna get some."

She didn't answer. Unsteady breath came and went through her mouth.

"You gonna get up and talk to Ma?"

"I, uh — Yes," she managed.

She rose unsteadily and began looking for something to put on. All her clothes were becoming uncomfortably tight. Finally she picked the uniform she had worn to work the day before. It smelled of stale perspiration, and there was a splash of catsup down the front of it that looked like blood. She shrugged into it, yanked up the zipper, and stopped with her hand on the door knob.

Talk to *her!* Talk to her?

Rachel was sitting straddle-legged, fat elbows on fat knees, while she fashioned a cigarette from a dog-eared package of Madonald's Fine Cut. Except for her eyes, which flicked once at Dolores and flicked swiftly away again, Dolores had no way of telling that Rachel knew that she had come into the room.

How can I talk to her? What am I supposed to say?

The silence grew, and grew.

Rachel lit her cigarette and puffed stolidly.

God! If I could only open that window. André's been promising for three days —

"How — How did you get into town?" she asked faintly.

Rachel giggled. "John Martineau."

"Oh?"

Who is John Martineau? And I don't know why she's laughing. Don't see anything funny.

There was another painful silence.

"Guess you're glad it's spring. Must be nice in the country, now."

"Yeah."

Silence.

All right! Don't talk, you stupid old cow —

Time ticked away.

Gee! Is André *never* coming? I gotta get that window open. I feel green.

She dragged a kitchen chair over and stood on the seat, pounding at the window sash with the heel of her hand. Rachel watched her with stolid indifference and continued to puff at her cigarette. The window gave way abruptly flying upwards and pinching Dolores' fingers.

"Ow! Oh, damn!"

Rachel stubbed her cigarette in a smear of egg yolk on an unwashed breakfast plate and began to roll another.

"How — How do you think André looks?" Dolores said desperately.

"Good."

As Dolores dragged the chair back to shove it under the table, she looked down into the part of Rachel's hair.

Lice! Dirty old bitch —

André walked in, a case of beer in his hand, followed by Isaac who carried another. Isaac set his case on the counter, ripped the top off it, and extracted four bottles. One after another, he removed the caps with his teeth. To Dolores his filthy teeth looked almost like tusks.

He took a swig from a bottle, and held one out to Dolores, making a wry face. "Goddamn teeth ain't so good no more. Gonna have to get me a bottle opener."

Dolores gulped sickly and stared at the top of the bottle he had handed to her.

Drink outta that after he's — ?

"Shoulda put the TV on for Ma, Dolly," André said, bending to turn the switch.

As the picture filled the screen, Isaac dragged the one vacant chair out from under the table, plopped onto it, leaned forward, and shoved the peak of his cap up. He took a long pull from his bottle, then belched resoundingly, never taking his eyes from the screen. Neither André nor Rachel paid the slightest attention.

André sat on the floor.

Where am I supposed to sit? Floor too, while that pair of dolts—? Well, André can darn well get them outta here. Lice! I'm not standing for—

Deliberately, she dumped the contents of the bottle of beer she was holding down the sink. Turning to André, she plucked at his sleeve and gestured with her head toward the door.

"Did you know they were coming?" she whispered when she had the door closed behind her.

"No, I — "

"Well, how're you gonna get rid of 'em? I can't stand — "

"Get rid of 'em? They're my folks. Maybe they'll stay a while."

"Stay?" Her voice arced upwards. "Sleep here? Where?"

"You and Ma take the bed. The old man and me'll sleep on the floor."

"Me sleep with — ? She's lousy, and she's probably got bed bugs!"

He giggled. "Hell! Little coal oil'll fix that."

"André — !"

He lifted one shoulder in a shrug, grinned at her, opened the door and went back into the suite. In the middle of the room he stopped and said over his shoulder, "You oughta go to the store, Dolly. Garlic sausage goes good with beer, and the folks ain't et today."

He spotted the sweater covering Gabriel Dumont's cage and removed it. "Jeez, Gaby! What's she doing to you?" he said, opening the cage door.

Gabriel squawked enquiringly, hopped through the door, and gyrated joyfully about the room, wings whistling, until he came to light on André's shoulder and demanded, "Goddamn it, André, gimme a kiss."

Television was forgotten. Rachel and Isaac doubled in helpless giggles. Isaac gestured toward the bird and said something in Cree. Rachel added something to his remark, and André answered them.

Talking Indian? Oh, *God!*

Several other unintelligible remarks passed between the three of them. At last André looked toward Dolores who was standing in the doorway. "You gonna get that sausage, Dolly? We're sure getting hungry."

"Sausage! If you want sausage, get it yourself. I'm going — " She snatched a jacket out of the closet at the entry and charged out of the suite.

She walked blindly through the warm late April sunlight. The coarse sand which had covered the treacherous winter streets still lay around unswept. Some of it got into her shoes and worked down under the tender soles of her feet. She scarcely felt it.

"My God!" she muttered from time to time. "My God, I never *knew* — "

She crossed Kingsway and stood in the rustling couch grass, clinging with both hands to the high wire fence of the Industrial Airport. Planes, large and small, landed and took off. She hardly saw them.

She looked with revulsion at her swelling belly. "I'd sooner it'd be like Astrid — dirty didies till it's twenty . . . Anything but like those bloody Indians." She burst into helpless tears, resting her forehead against the cold, unyielding wire of the fence.

If I could talk to Mama — Or even Thorvald. But what could they do? Nothing. Daddy — ? She shuddered. Breeds! If he knew —

Thought I had it made. Thought I was so smart. So what if André *was* a breed? Once he got through that course at NAIT and got a job we were gonna — Even if I had to steal to do it, but — All he can do is howl about being cooped-up in classes. Never saw him so happy as he was slopping beer with those lousy old —

Lousy's right. "Hell! Little coal oil'll fix that," she mocked.

The baby stirred.

Why didn't I have brains enough to get rid of it away back?

Distractedly she wandered back and forth along the stretch of couch grass, not noticing how the day was darkening and chilling; an early spring thunder storm was brewing.

A sudden gust of wind plastered her inadequate clothes to her body and chilled her through and through. Thunder boomed, and wind-driven icy rain penetrated to her skin. With teeth clenched against her shivering, and sheltering her face with one hand, she crossed the throughfare and scuttled along through the rain under the wind-tossed trees.

When she entered the suite her clothes were dripping, and her hair hung in sodden strings. Her stomach was revolted by the reek of cigarette smoke.

André tore his gaze away from the television long enough to remark, "Little wet out there, huh?"

She flung into the bathroom, not knowing whether to vomit first and strip her clothes after, or strip her clothes and then vomit. The first of the two alternatives became imperative.

Still gasping and wiping her eyes, she flung her clothes into the bathtub and put on an old terrycloth robe. Her hands were so numb she had difficulty tying the cord. Barefooted, she padded through the kitchen. Rachel, swaying slightly on the chair, watched her with dull eyes. Isaac lay full length on the bed, snoring. A trickle of spittle ran out of one corner of his mouth and onto the pillow. The black rubbers on his feet rested side by side on the clean white chenille bedspread.

Dolores flew at him, fists and fingernails. "Damn you! Out of my bed! Out! Out! *Out!*"

With a bewildered grunt, Isaac stumbled to his feet, raising his arm to protect his face.

André grabbed Dolores and dragged her away. "What the hell! Dolly, you gone nuts?"

Rachel, her mouth slack, dropped a cigarette butt to the floor, to join several others which ringed her chair.

"Look at her! Both of them," Dolores stormed. "Pigs!" She kicked furiously at a half-full bottle of beer. It spiralled away, spilling its contents through the cigarette butts.

"Dirty white bitch," Rachel muttered, heading for the door.

Isaac, blinking bewilderment, and not walking quite straight, followed her up the stairs.

"Ma, just a second — Listen," André begged.

Isaac and Rachel went out of the door into the pelting rain without looking back.

"Ma! Ma, listen — !"

The only answer was the click of the spring-loaded aluminium door closing itself.

André cast Dolores a look of desperation and black fury before he grabbed a jacket and pounded after them.

"Yeah. Go! You useless goddamn breed. Daddy was right all along. I shoulda known—" Dolores screamed.

Gabriel Dumont, terrified by the uproar, flew madly about the room. Dolores batted at him again and again. Puffing, exhausted, and confused, he landed at last on the terrycloth robe covering her forearm. She grabbed him. He bit her once, very hard, before she wrung his neck. She flung his body down into the pool of spilled beer and cigarette butts.

Half an hour later, Dolores stumbled out of a taxi in front of the Medical Arts Building. The receptionist in the doctor's office was buttoning her coat preparing to leave for the night.

"Mrs. Macgregor, isn't it? Is — Is something wrong?"

"Gotta see the doctor. Right now."

The woman hesitated. "I think perhaps you'd better wait in his private office. I'll — I'll speak to him."

She made a gesture toward an open door. Dolores stumbled into the room and collapsed into a chair.

The doctor sat quietly, his eyes averted, and his expression sad, while Dolores poured out hysteria and tears. When she had calmed down a little he sighed, rubbed at one corner of his mouth with his open palm and scratched the back of his head.

"Now, m'dear, I'm sure you know that an abortion at this stage is absolutely out of the question. If you really don't want your child you can put it up for adoption at birth. At the moment, you are too upset to make a rational decision. You have almost five months to think about it. Right now—" He looked at her, lips pursed, eyebrows arched, then reached for the phone. "I'm going to put you in hospital for a few days. Just until you calm down and gather yourself together."

twenty-three

André stood in the mud beside Isaac and Rachel on the edge of Highway 28 leading north. The rain beat on his back while his parents faced into it, thumbs extended to the traffic. They ignored him. Rain dripped from their coats and made tear-trickles down their brown, seamed faces.

An ancient Oldsmobile, already loaded with Indians slithered to a stop. Isaac and Rachel crowded into the car; it roared away leaving André standing in the pelting rain.

Numbly, he turned back toward the city. He was shaking with cold. Half an hour later he was sheltering under the eaves of the garage in the back of the Sawchuck yard.

Go down into that goddamn hole in the ground? And Dolly? Jeez! I — I —

He was shivering uncontrollably before he could make himself enter the house. At the bottom of the stairs the door of the rooms was wide open. The place was in darkness. He snapped on the light. Unwashed dishes, cigarette butts, and beer bottles — And a bundle of jewel-blue feathers lying in a pool of spilled beer.

"Gaby? Oh, jeez — Gaby! The bitch. The stinkin' bitch!"

He scooped the tiny wet bundle into the palm of his hand and cupped it there. Then, with exaggerated gentleness he laid it on top of a calculus text on the table.

The walls crowded in on him. He made false starts toward the bedroom, the bathroom, and the stairs leading outside.

Get out! Now! Before she comes, or —

He ripped out of his wet clothes, buttons popping and scattering, then pawed into dry ones in a clumsy, unthinking rush. He scooped a small tower of coins from the top of the bureau and dropped them into his pocket. For a second he hesitated, then snatched the drawer open and took a twenty dollar bill from the envelope Dolores had hidden there. He closed his eyes and held out his palms to ward off the threatening walls.

The alarm clock clacked smugly. He grabbed it and on his way through the kitchen smashed it against the door of the refrigerator. At the top of the stairs he almost collided with Mrs. Sawchuck, returning from a two-day visit to her sister in Vegreville. She stared at him suspiciously. He ducked past her and fled into the new night and the chilly, slanting rain.

He walked with no plan except the need to put distance between Dolores, the rooms, and himself. By the time he was in downtown Edmonton his clothes were soaked again. He felt sick and miserable.

There's no damn way I'm goin' back there, but what the hell *am* I gonna do?

He backed into the sheltering doorway of a store and stood there, shuddering with cold. The odd pedestrian scuttled past, face averted from the rain. The asphalt streets gleamed with water and the brilliant reflections of passing car lights. A lighted phone booth stood on the corner. André stared at it for a long time before he plucked up the courage to enter it. His hands were so cold that he could scarcely fit a dime into the slot.

Maybe Bayrocks'd let me stay for a couple of days. Maybe if I could just talk to 'em —

He tried the number three times. There was no answer.

Musta gone someplace. Maybe after a while — Jeez! I gotta find *someplace* to get warm. Only three blocks over to 97th Street. Go into a hotel outta the fucking rain. Couple of beers—

The place was crowded and stank of cigarette smoke and damp wool. André slipped into a corner with his back to the wall. He ordered two glasses of beer, promising himself that when he had finished drinking them he would try Bayrocks' number again. He felt light-headed. He had had nothing to eat that day except two slices of toast and an egg for breakfast and the garlic sausage he had eaten with the beer.

Should go into a café, maybe, but — Nah! I'm just startin' to get warm. After I finish this beer.

He was setting down the second glass, empty, when a red-faced guy at the next table called for more beer for his five companions. He peered blearily at André and roared, "Hey, kid! Why the hell you sittin' there lookin' like you lost your last friend?" He hooked an empty chair with the toe of his boot and dragged it in beside him. "C'mon, sit in," he ordered, then told the bar-tender, "Couple more for my friend, here."

"Thanks, but — "

"What the hell, buddy? I said, *sit in*."

Spoilin' for a fight. I better drink one glass with him, and then —

But by the time he had finished the glass it didn't seem to matter any more. He bought a round for his new friends. He tried to remember something that he had planned to do, but it kept slipping away from him. There were blurred images of faces, and a great deal of silly laughter at stories that he did not understand. He only intended to put his head down on his arms for a moment —

When he came to, he was being bounced along in the back seat of a crew cab. His head was flopping helplessly. His neck felt as if it had been broken and he was wedged between two of his drinking buddies who were arguing about cars. The man who had invited him to drink with them in the first place was driving the truck down a rough country road.

"Gotta puke," André gulped.

The truck stopped. André scrambled over his companions, wrestled the door open and made it to the edge of the ditch. It was still raining.

Beer! God, I dunno where I put it all. No wonder I—

When he could retch no more he climbed back in the truck. The driver didn't even look around. He let out the clutch and they continued to crawl along the rain-slick road.

Finally they pulled into a field where some aluminium construction trailers and several earth-moving machines were standing in the rain.

The driver stumbled out of the truck and said, "C'mon, boys. Party's over. Let's get some shut-eye."

The men got out of the truck. Sober and fully awake now, André followed the last straggler into a trailer and stood shivering as the other men fell into bunks.

The red-faced man sat on the edge of a bunk with his pants crumpled around his feet squinting at André as though seeing him for the first time.

"How the hell did you get here?"

"Dunno. Don't remember — "

The man's hands hung helplessly between his thighs and there was an air of unutterable weariness about him. "Well, for christsake — " He sighed and gestured toward an empty bunk. "We lost Scotty somewheres. Climb into his sack and we'll get it sorted out in the morning."

André tried to spread his clothes to dry when he took them off, then eased into the strange bed smelling of stale sweat and Brut shaving lotion.

He wakened to the shuffling of feet, the smell of tobacco smoke, and the mutter of voices. He opened his eyes. Four of the men were sitting around a table playing cards. Rain poured down the window. André sat up. One of the guys glanced at him. "Hi. How d'ya feel?"

"Head's busted."

"After the beer you put away last night it oughtta be." He grinned good-naturedly. "Go take a leak, then head for the cook house. We talked Sarah into savin' you some breakfast."

André scrambled out of bed and began dressing. "Where — How will I get back to town?"

"You're in luck," the red-faced guy said. "Can't work today 'cause it's rainin'. I'll run you in myself after you've et."

Out in the yard André looked about. There were two trenchers, great piles of sewer tile, loads of planking, and seas of yellow-grey mud.

As he headed for the outdoor biffy he remembered the money he had taken from the drawer the night before, but when he thrust his hands into his pockets the only thing that he found there was a ball of lint. He fished it out and looked at it ruefully. He was diffident about entering the other trailer which he knew must be the cook house, but he was hungry. When he did he saw a middle-aged female, belly out-thrust beneath a dirty apron, washing dishes at the table.

"Yer grub's in the oven, and make it snappy, will ya?" she muttered. "Pretty soon be dinner time."

The pancakes were dried to the consistency of leather and the sausages burned, but André ate every scrap of them. He rose, plate and cutlery in hand and offered them to the dishwasher. She ignored him, craning her neck to see through the window.

"There's the old man."

"Who?"

"Old Sandon. Owns the outfit." She laughed. "Bet he's doin' some fancy cussin'. Rainin', and the crew sittin' around on their butts — "

André came up behind her and looked out. A tall old man dressed in a shabby business suit stood in the yard. Everything about him was grey; his clothes, his skin, and the silver stubble on his chin. He wore a waspish expression and his lips moved continuously.

"Yeah, he's cussin'. Just look at him," Sarah marvelled. Sandon made for the cook house. "Oh, oh! Comin' for his coffee and I'm gonna get an earful of—" She broke off, eyes widening as she looked at André. "Jesus! What am I gonna do with you?"

"Huh?"

"Sandon don't feed bums. He'd fire Rusty if he knew he'd brung you here." She snatched the plate and cutlery from his hands and dropped them into the dishpan. "Sit down, and remember you just got here five minutes ago." She slopped a mugful of coffee from a pot on the stove and set it in front of him singing out as she did so, "Come on in, Mr. Sandon. Coffee's hot."

Sandon entered the cook house and stood with the door in his hand while he gestured outside and demanded dramatically, "You ever see the beat of that, Sarah? Terror to hell! Start out like that in the spring and she's liable to rain clean till freeze-up. I don't know what a man's to do, by God I don't. I recall in 1927 — " He spotted André and broke off.

"Young fella's lookin' for a job, Mr. Sandon," Sarah said. "Knew you'd be along pretty quick, so I figured it'd be all right if I give him a cuppa coffee."

Job? Who the hell — ? Well, why not? Yeah! And to hell with Dolly and that goddamn school.

"Job, eh?" Sandon looked André up and down, eyes narrowed, lips compressed. "We've got a full crew here, but—Did you ever string barbed wire?"

"Helped a guy one time for a coupla days."

"I bought a little acreage out west of town. Going to keep a couple of ponies out there for my grandchildren. I'll take Dave off the outfit here tomorrow and you and he can fence the place. That's if you want the job."

Barbed wire — Bitch of a job, but I ain't got a red cent, so — "Would I be livin' in camp here?"

"That's right. We knock your board off your wages. I'll be taking the two of you out to the acreage in the morning and fetching you back at night."

After Sandon had gone André realized he hadn't thought to ask what he was being paid.

By noon the next day his back and shoulders burned with the agony of twisting a post-hole auger and then heaving the implement loaded with dirt out of the holes he dug. Dave, his fellow worker, an intense, taciturn young man, as lean and hard as the fence posts he wrestled, drove himself and André without mercy. When he called a halt at noon, André flopped in the shade of a spruce tree and gingerly examined the blisters on his hands.

"Jeez, I'm beat! Ain't worked that hard since—" He glanced up. Dave was grinning.

So I never worked that hard. Not with my hands. Bastard thinks he's so hot. Like to see him wrestle some of them physics problems at NAIT. By Christ, he'd find out — God, I dunno — Maybe I'm a damn fool. Maybe I ought to ask old Sandon to drop me off in Edmonton tonight. Go patch it up with Dolly and head for classes in the morning.

Yeah? Fucking jailhouse — and Dolly — And her fucking TV — Sooner have blisters on my hands the size of mallards' eggs.

He ate thick roast beef sandwiches in silence and drank coffee from a thermos, then stretched out in the sun and tried to make his twitching muscles relax. Frogs sang in a nearby slough. The sun and wind was sweet to his face. He wakened to Dave kicking him none too gently on the sole of his boot. "C'mon, Tecumseh, hour's up."

"Name's André."

"No kiddin'? From the way you was hobblin' around I figured it might be Chief Dan George."

Bastard! I'll keep up with him, and to hell with the blisters.

By five-thirty he was stumbling when he walked. The palms of his hands were bloody and raw and his back so sore he could hardly lift the auger.

"Well, you pullin' out now or after supper?" Dave asked as he gathered up the tools while they waited for Mr. Sandon to come and get them.

"Get off my back, goddamn it!"

"If you're figurin' on stayin' you better dig through the garbage and find yourself a big tin can to use for a pee pot," Dave said in an almost kindly tone. "Soak them hands in it to toughen 'em up. I'm not kiddin'. Fastest way to toughen a soft pair of hands."

"Yeah?" André giggled. "Well, if it works —"

If his first day on the fencing job was bad, the second was worse. But by the third even his hands were beginning to toughen up. After supper that night he took the tin can off into the bush and sat down with his back against a poplar tree out of sight of the rest of the crew. A pair of blue birds were flashing back and forth across the little clearing.

Same colour as Gaby. Jeez, he was a cute little bugger! That goddamn Dolly — If — if she'd wring Gaby's neck, what about the — the kid?

The night the fencing was finished Mr. Sandon said, "Fella quit on me today, André. Shovel tickles his hands. Are you interested in the job?"

"Yeah. Be all right."

The job consisted of lowering lengths of vitreous tile sewer pipe on a rope eight feet down into a ditch where a pipe layer joined the lengths together. Compared to stringing barbed wire it was a soft touch.

Late in the afternoon it began to rain. Rusty, the foreman, shut the job down. André started to follow the rest of the crew who were straggling off towards the trailer when Rusty called him back to pile up some scattered pipe, so that a bulldozer could manoeuver to backfill some of the ditch the next morning. While André was busy at this task Rusty prowled along the edge of the ditch staring down into it.

"Ground don't look right," he grumbled, "and if she rains hard tonight—" He turned to André. "Gimme a hand here. I'm gonna knock this shorin' out and move it a coupla feet closer to the machine." Stepping on the struts spreading the planks apart, he climbed down into the ditch. He looked up at André and ordered, "Take that plank that's layin' up there and knock the struts out for me."

André did as he was bidden. Rusty shifted one length of plank into a new position and was turning to lift the other when suddenly the earth caved out of the bank where the plank had stood, burying him to the knees. He could not move. He looked up at André, his face the colour of bread dough. "For christsake, help me."

André scrambled down the shoring and grabbed a shovel. He was not particularly aware of danger as he dug and clawed earth from around Rusty's legs.

Then he grabbed Rusty by one arm and yanked him free. "Back between the shorin'! *Move!*" Rusty gasped.

André sprang for it with Rusty on his heels. With a mumbling roar the whole ditch caved in upon itself. Eight feet of sandy soil covered where they had stood seconds before.

The crew appeared, bug-eyed, and shouting senseless orders to each other. Thirty times between then and bedtime Rusty expounded to anyone who would listen how André had saved his life. André protested again and again that he hadn't even known enough to be aware of danger, but nobody listened.

Sandon's outfit were hard-working, hard-drinking construction types. From Monday morning to Saturday noon they wrestled pipe and plank and earth; from Saturday noon to Sunday night they wrestled beer bottles, broads, and hangovers. They took André to their hearts. He became one of the boys. He never thought of Dolores except when he jerked from sleep in the dead of night after dreaming about her.

One Saturday afternoon toward the end of August he and Dave decided that they needed new outfits of work clothes. They visited the Army and Navy department store to get that business out of the way before the Saturday revels began. André was pocketing his change and reflecting ruefully that he had very little money to show for his summer's work. Two aisles over he saw Dolores, huge now with pregnancy. His heart stumbled. Her face was drawn and her long hair stringy, as though it was a long time since it had been washed. She was listening with a slack mouth and a deferential air to Essie, who was telling her something with an intense expression on her scarred face.

Dolly! With that bitch. Jeez! Look at the belly on her. Well, it's the end of August next week. Less than a month and the kid'll be — Oh, Christ!

He gulped and his hands began to quiver. Rapidly he walked

toward the door where Dave was waiting for him.

"What's wrong, André?"

"Dunno, I—Listen, Dave, how about dumpin' my stuff back in the truck, will ya? I feel kinda shitty. Guess I'll hitch back to camp."

For a week fierce inner arguments drove him this way and that, but it always came back to the same thing. I'd give half my ass if I never had to look at Dolly again, but that's my kid she's got in her belly.

He no longer played cards with the crew after supper, but wandered about the construction site, stopping again and again to stare at the towering buildings of Edmonton that showed dove grey in the twilight three miles away.

Wonder if Dolly's still living in them rooms? If she's took off and I can't find her I'll never know—Jeez! Hanging around with that goddamn Essie. *She's* trouble, and Dolly's so — Maybe Dolly's broke! Thieving again to —

In an hour's time he was lying belly down in the Sawchuck yard, peering through a slit in the curtains down into the basement rooms. He was weak with relief when he saw Dolores slumped in a chair, biting her fingernails and staring at television. He sneaked around to the mailbox and dropped an envelope into it with her name scrawled across it. It contained nearly two hundred dollars.

"But what's that gonna fix, slippin' her money?" he thought as he headed back to camp. Sure, it might keep her outta the slammer till after the kid's born, but then what? No damn way she gets her claws into me again. Ever. But what about the kid? Poor little bugger. When I think of how Dodie Rose treated her kid, and I ain't so sure she wasn't more human than Dolly. Christ! I dunno—I just dunno—Would Dolly even have brains enough to hold him when he hollers?

He avoided the crew and became spooky and withdrawn. Many times during that month he sneaked into the city at night to check on Dolores. In the cook house joking remarks passed back and forth across the breakfast table about him yelling in his sleep. His concentration slipped. He left a truck in neutral while he got out to throw some shoring out of the way. The truck rolled, hit a stack of sewer pipe and sent it tumbling down into the open ditch.

Rusty bawled him out. The next day he sent André in the

truck to get a number of things from the storage yard including a couple of wheel barrows for hauling cement. He forgot the wheel barrows. Rusty cussed him out in front of the whole crew, slammed into the truck and went back to get them himself.

"Hell! He think I done it on purpose?"

"What's eatin' ya anyhow?" Dave probed, "You been as useless as a pinch of coon shit ever since — "

"None of your goddamn business!"

Dave lifted one shoulder in a shrug. "Well, screw you, buster." He stalked off to join the rest of the crew who were rolling smokes. They presented a solid wall of back to André.

Yeah. Make the guys sore at me. That's real smart! *But the fucking trouble is I dunno what to do.* Damn near the end of September. Suppose the next time I go looking for Dolly she's gone? Christ! I might never find out what happened to my kid.

On Thursday night Rusty told him to put a wooden plug in the sewer pipe already laid in the ditch. He forgot. That night it rained, and in the morning the pipe was half full of mud. Rusty fired him.

twenty-four

He tromped along the muddy road toward Edmonton. Gumbo and dead leaves stuck to his work boots. It was Friday. The unlucky day, Sister Bridget had once laughingly called it. André knew she had only spoken in whimsy, but Fridays always made him uneasy. It was cold and overcast. Ice covered the pools in the ditches beside the road, and only the top few leaves still clung to the poplar trees. He carried his spare clothes in a flour sack with a picture of Robin Hood on it that Sarah had given him.

Rain had washed mud out of the gravel on the road, so that there were spots where the stones were shining clean. From force of habit he stopped to scuff out those that interested him. He picked up a specimen sparkling with fool's gold and turned it in his labour-toughened hands.

Rocks! You crazy bastard, they're all in your head. Just like Ma said.

He pitched the stone full force and watched it disturb the branches of a spruce tree far over in a field.

One thing I know for damn sure, I gotta find another job. I'm going straight to Manpower as soon as I get in town. Them guys was saying at supper last night that jobs is getting scarce again. I hope I can —

On the outskirts of the city he spotted a bus-stop sign. He waited beside it watching the odd snowflake drift toward the earth. When he saw the bus coming he began searching his pockets for change.

"All I got is dollars," he told the driver, giggling with embarrassment.

"Yeah, I've noticed you guys have a lot of trouble that way."
The door snapped shut in André's face and the bus pulled away.

"Hell with that bastard. Bet *he* ain't got damn near his whole
month's wages in his pocket."

He stepped out onto the street and stuck out his thumb. No
car stopped for him.

Guess nobody's gonna. I look like an old construction stiff on
the bum. I'll hoof it. Gotta find someplace to stay. Get washed
and cleaned up.

His journey from the outskirts of the city to the centre, where
the Manpower office was located, took him within a few blocks
of the Sawchuck house. He fully intended to pass by, but anxi-
ety drove him to chance going down the alley behind the house,
in the hope that he might see some reassuring sign that Dolly
was still there. What he saw was anything but reassuring. Hanging on the clothes line were two cotton mats which had been on
the floors in the rooms, and a pair of curtains which André had
opened and closed a hundred times.

The old lady's cleaning out — Dolly's gone! Oh, Jesus — ! I
gotta go in there and — And ask —

He stared at the house trying to screw up his courage. Finally
he opened the gate and slipped in beside the garage where he
stood partially concealed by a crab apple tree still laden with
frozen fruit. He could not summon the courage to go to the door.
It was a relief when Mrs. Sawchuck, a grim expression on her
broad, red face, and a pail in her hand, slammed out of the house.
She plodded down the steps and fired the water under the tree
where André was standing, barely missing his boots.

"You!"

"Where's — Dolly here?"

"She better not show her face around here again. I dunno
where you get the nerve, either."

"You — You know where she is?"

"All I know is that scar-faced little tramp she hangs around
with — Essie, ain't it? Well, she showed up here to pick up
Dolores' stuff. How d'ya like that? Kinda thanks I get. Felt sorry
for Dolores when you run out on her. Looked after her like she
was my own kid, and that's the thanks I get—Day she gets outta
hospital she sends somebody else to pick up her stuff! Left the
rooms lookin' like a herd of pigs had — "

"Hospital? The — the kid?"

"Kid! Whadda you care? You run out on him before he was born. She give him away like he was a mongrel pup. Great pair, you two. Godalmighty! Can't look after a budgie bird."

"*Give him away*? Where — ? Who — ?"

"That Essie says she put him up for adoption."

"*Where*? I gotta know."

She tipped the pail to drain the last drops of grey water out of it. "Go pester somebody else. Royal Alex Hospital, maybe. And get outta my yard. Come nosin' around here again and I'll call the cops."

André was a block and a half down the street before he realized that he was not exactly sure where the hospital was. He pounded up to an old man digging a flower bed to ask directions. Before he answered, the old fellow backed up to stand beside an Alsatian dog which was staked out on the lawn. André could still hear the dog roaring as he raced on into the next block.

He puffed to a sweaty halt outside the forbidding complex of yellow brick buildings and started reading signs.

"Womens' Pavilion"—Guess that's where Dolly'd be. If she's here. Dunno what the hell I'm gonna say to her. If there was a way I could sneak in there and grab that kid — Grab the kid! Christ! I gotta be crazy. Touch him, even if he is mine, and I'd have every Mountie in the country chasin' me. And what'd I *do* with a kid? Nah! I gotta go in there and ask to—Jesus, I dunno— But I gotta.

He hesitated for a long time beside a bed of frozen, red geraniums. He was trembling and he sighed repeatedly. Slowly he began walking down the ramp marked "Admitting".

A Yellow Cab passed him, pulled into the ambulance entrance, and stopped. The glass doors of the hospital opened. André heard a familiar giggle. He caught his breath. Dolores, followed by Essie, passed not ten feet from him and hopped into the cab.

"Little medicine bundle!" Dolores cackled. "Gee, Essie, you're comical. Wow! Was I glad to get rid of it."

Essie handed a suitcase to the cabbie for him to load. "Well, I *guess*. Anyhow, that's that. Now, we got it all set up for us, Dolly baby, and it don't include any howlin' brats."

The cab pulled out of the hospital grounds and was turning onto Kingsway Avenue before André moved.

Jeez! I shoulda stopped her, but she never took the kid. He's gotta be in here. Somewheres —

He went into the admitting office and tried to summon the courage to speak to a young receptionist who was typing some forms. She looked up and smiled. "Can I help you?"

"Nah! I just — " He rounded a corner out of her sight and stared about him helplessly.

An intern in a white suit and with a gauze mask hanging loose about his neck hurried along the corridor. He looked sharply at André. The doors of an elevator opened to discharge passengers. André ducked into it. He frowned at the floor buttons, shrugged, and pushed number two. He was skulking along the corridor trying to formulate something to say at one of the nursing stations when he came to a window. Beyond the window he saw a baby, snugly wrapped and lying in a metal and plastic bassinette. He stopped and stared into the clenched, perfect little face. In the same room, too far away for him to see clearly, five other babies were bundled in bassinettes.

A nurse in the room caught sight of him, smiled, came to the door and asked, "What baby would you like to see?"

His heart was hammering. "The—the Macgregor kid." Bluff, but she might —

The nurse looked at him keenly. "Macgregor?" There was a pause. "That child has already been taken to the crèche."

"Huh?" He gulped.

"Well, you see, the Child Welfare takes them if the mother gives them up for adoption."

"Child Welfare? Where — ?"

"Who are you?"

"The kid's old man. Where do I go to see my kid?"

"I'll get somebody to take you downstairs to talk to the social worker, Mr. — Mr. Macgregor. She'll be able to answer your questions."

The guide left André in a small outer office where he crouched in a chair wishing miserably that he had tobacco and cigarette papers. On the other side of the door he could hear a woman's voice, calm and reassuring, and the higher-pitched tearful voice of a girl. From time to time there was the staccato clatter of a typewriter. A white-suited porter pushed a stretcher along a corridor outside. By craning his neck André could see the face of a patient, still deep in anesthesia.

The palms of André's hands began to sweat and he looked quickly away. The porter and his patient disappeared. The corridor was empty.

What am I getting myself into? If I had any brains I'd be down that corridor and out the door before—Might be the best thing a guy like me can ever do for his kid.

What am I gonna say when they open that door and call me in? "He's my kid. None of your damn business suppose I pack him around in my hip pocket or hang him in a tree while I wrestle pipe on a construction job?" He snorted. That'd go over real big! Jecz, if—If—Suppose I took him up to Ma? He shook his head. No good. He wouldn't have been a heck of a lot worse off if Dolly'd kept him.

Nellie! A grin slowly spread over his face. He rubbed his sweating palms up and down his thighs.

"Nellie Bayrock—Jeez! I wonder . . .

twenty-five

That December the weather was rough, even by Edmonton standards. On Christmas Eve André clung to a bar on a crowded bus which swayed down 109th Street. His clothes stank. He avoided the eyes of other passengers, who glanced at him distastefully, then edged away. When the bus turned a corner he pulled the bell cord, pushed his way to the back door and stepped down into the trampled snow. The cold set his eyes watering. He ducked his head away from the slight stirring of south-east wind and shifted the parcel he carried from the crook of one arm to the crook of the other.

Froze my damn nose again today. Fifth time this month. Well, it's a job. It pays, and they can't say I don't work at it.

He could hear Ronnie practising his trumpet when he was still half a block away from the Bayrock house. He giggled. Jeez! I hope Nellie don't make him practise Christmas day.

He rounded the house, opened the back door, scuttled down the stairs and ducked into the little bathroom where he shucked his dirty clothes and turned on the shower. When he had towelled himself and dressed in a pair of clean levis and an old sweater, he packed his dirty clothes into the automatic washer and switched it on. Then, with a glow of anticipation, he picked up the parcel he had brought and headed up the stairs.

Sam, who was reading the newspaper in the living room, peered at him over his glasses. "Well, how's the city's garbage business today?"

"Rough. And it'll get rougher when we start picking up Christmas trees next week."

"There's a fella talking about quitting at the plant. Chance I might get you on at the end of January."

"Yeah? Be great, but I ain't countin' chickens. One thing about garbage, there's always lots of it."

Nellie stuck her head around the doorway of the kitchen and looked at him. "If you don't take time off to heal that nose or else start wearing the balaclava I knitted for you, you're going to be the only garbage collector in Edmonton without a nose."

"Child Welfare guys say I gotta be a workin' man."

"Yeah, but they didn't say you had to be a martyr."

"Ah, might warm up next week. Give my nose a chance to heal."

"Had a visitor today," she said as she began laying cutlery on the dining room table. "Social worker checking up on you and Gaby."

"'Yeah?" He waited, heart quickening.

"Real pleased. He says if you keep on the way you're going there's no reason you won't get the adoption papers in a year."

He snorted. "Heck of a thing! Adoptin' your own kid — "

He went to the crib and grinned at the baby, who squirmed with delight at the sight of him. "Hey, ya old stinker, how's she usin' you today?" He bent and blew softly on the baby's bare, brown belly. Gaby crowed a hiccupy laugh of delight.

"You laughed! By gosh, for that you get your teddy bear a whole day early." He had started to strip the paper from his parcel when Dick appeared with a ring binder in his hands.

"André, will you take a look at this dumb question? My solution is out by a mile, and I can't figure — "

André laid the teddy bear aside and picked Gaby up. With the baby straddling his hip, he read over Dick's shoulder. "Looks to me like you went wrong there." He pointed to Dick's work. "Now, go back to your tables and you'll see — "

Dick clapped his head. "How dumb can I get?" He looked searchingly at André. "Man! I can't figure out why you don't get yourself rounded up and go back to NAIT."

"A guy's gotta work three years before Manpower'll pay the shot. And I dunno — " He laughed. "Might find myself a real woman and have another couple of little sonsaguns like Gaby before then."

"Funny you never run into Dolores," Nellie remarked.

"Oh, I run into her. And I kept right on runnin' before she spotted me."

"You did? Where?"

"Greasy spoon downtown."

Wiggling her ass for some character outta the bush with a fistful of cash. Poor old Dolly. Next thing it'll be a white Gary One Blanket, and after that — He shrugged mentally. Clara?

"Guess I'm kinda mushy," Nellie said, "but I always feel sorry she wouldn't even look at Gaby before she put him up for adoption."

"Good thing!" André snorted, "She mighta wrung his neck. He's the spittin' image of my old man. Shoulda called you Isaac instead of Gabriel Joseph, shouldn't we, kid? Nobody's ever gonna take you for a dark white fella."

"Won't hurt him for work," Nellie said dryly. She surveyed the table. "All right, everybody. Supper's ready. Let's sit in. Do you want to put Gaby back in his crib, André?"

Gaby squawked once when André laid him down, then grabbed at one of his waving feet with both hands. It eluded him. He blinked and tried again.

"Hey!" André crowed, "Gaby found his feet."

"Good for him." Nellie detoured from the kitchen with a steaming bowl of carrots in her hands and stood beside him smiling down at the baby. "More than you can say for most of the rest of us."

"Huh?"

"Us Métis — Haven't found our feet. Yet. Well, give us time. When you stop to think, that kid's only the sixth, or maybe seventh generation of a new race."

"Maybe Gaby finds 'em."

"Maybe. Him or his grandson. Might learn to stand on them, or even run. Long as he doesn't try it with a gum boot on one foot and a moccasin on the other."